MW00908437

Dee Harrison-Schultz is a licensed clinical counselor for the past 25 years. She is experienced in working with a variety of disorders, within the prison system, as well as in an outpatient setting. These experiences sparked an intense curiosity in forensics and criminology. *Darwin Was Right* is her premier novel. She lives with her husband, David Schultz, and their two rescue dogs, Zeke and Zoe. They currently divide their time between Spruce Pine, North Carolina, and Punta Gorda, Florida.

I dedicate this book to my beloved husband, David. Without his help and support, his patience and understanding, this endeavor would never have been possible. Also many thanks to my friends and family who always had my back.

Denise Harrison

DARWIN WAS RIGHT

AUSTIN MACAULEY PUBLISHERS™

LONDON • CAMBRIDGE • NEW YORK • SHARJAH

Ordering Information
Quantity sales: Special discounts are available on quantity purchases by corporations, associations, and others. For details, contact the publisher at the address below.

Publisher's Cataloging-in-Publication data
Harrison, Denise
Darwin Was Right

ISBN 9781638297659 (Paperback)
ISBN 9781638297666 (ePub e-book)

Library of Congress Control Number: 2022919015

www.austinmacauley.com/us

First Published 2022
Austin Macauley Publishers LLC
40 Wall Street, 33rd Floor, Suite 3302
New York, NY 10005
USA

mail-usa@austinmacauley.com
+1 (646) 5125767

My interest in forensic psychology and the criminal psyche began at a rather early age. I have recollections of watching crime dramas as a young adult, and while they did entertain me, I always felt like something was missing. To me, the missing component was the "why". It was not enough for me to view the behaviors, the investigations, the pursuit and the eventual apprehending of the perpetrator. I needed to know what the motivation was behind the heinous acts, what was the attacker thinking, or hope to accomplish. Basically I wondered what created this monster? Did he or she come out of the womb like this? Were they a product of their environment? Were there other factors that needed consideration?

Over the years the television and movie industry appeared to recognize the need that many of us had for this additional component. Many started addressing this factor, with my favorite being the television show *Criminal Minds*. This series centered around the motivation and psychopathology of the men and women committing the crimes. I was devastated when it went off the air.

I owe much gratitude to my dear friends who have supported me in my endeavors, and who have always offered encouragement. Shout outs to Tina Burnette, Pam Timmins, and many others. One of my biggest supporters has been my mother, Doris Laurange, who always has been there for me. Last, but certainly not least, I never would have even tried to undertake this without the unconditional love and support from the love of my life, David Schultz.

Chapter 1

Striding purposefully out of the somewhat dismal concrete building which served as her place of employment, the beautiful young woman luxuriated in the warm embrace of the sun on her skin. After hours of sitting at her desk, staring at the blinding light of her computer screen, being outside felt like an oasis of cool water would to a nomad lost in a vast desert. Emmanuelle Ariana Blanchet, known to most friends and acquaintances as Emmie, worked at Quantico as an FBI Profiler for the past three years. Despite being a relative rookie, Emmie's reputation, for being able to rapidly and accurately get into a killer's mind and anticipate their next move, was uncanny. That talent, along with her command of nine languages, her insightfulness when interviewing suspects and witnesses, and her warm manner that instantly makes others comfortable had earned her a position as Supervisory Agent over her team of fellow profilers.

Emmie often said that she owed everything to her parents. The only child of a highly educated and multi-cultural couple, she was raised with many advantages. Her mother Chloe was half Indian and half French, while her father André was French with dual citizenship in both the

U.S. and France. With her mother traveling around the world for her career as a classical musician, and her father holding a busy top position at Interpol, Emmie was often sent to her grandparent's chateau in France, where she spent her mornings with a private tutor and her afternoons frolicking on the acres and acres of manicured lawns and flowering pastures on the estate. At the age of fifteen, she entered university as an early enrollee and graduated with her Ph.D. in Criminology at twenty-three. Her reputation spread quickly, and three days after graduation, she was recruited into the FBI as a profiler and a couple of short years later, she was promoted to supervisor.

As she was enjoying her brief respite outside, her cell phone jarred her back from her quiet reverie with the familiar alert of a text message. Looking down, she recognized the caller as her technical assistant, Sarah. Swiping to open, she read, "Emmie, we need you back at the office. We have a case." Although she was somewhat disappointed that her brief break was over, she still felt that well-known surge of anticipation that she always experienced when she knew her unique skill set was getting ready for a challenge.

As she walked into the suite of offices reserved for her department, she saw her staff already there and waiting. Emmie had hand-selected her team. She had the utmost confidence in every member's unique attributes and strong dedication to her and the work that they all performed. They were a motley crew, who all fit together perfectly like a jigsaw puzzle, in spite of their different backgrounds, skills, and personalities. Sarah Thomas served as Emmie's direct assistant, as well as the technical expert and often a buffer for the Press. Raj Patel was Emmie's father's closest friend, had served with him at Interpol and Homeland Security. He had retired at the age of fifty to write a couple of crime novels but missing the action of the field, he came to work for the FBI a few years later. Shawn O'Brian, an ex-Navy Seal, had worked for the agency for fifteen years and with this team for a year. Kaitlyn Jackson was a former DC homicide detective. Robert Montgomery was recruited from his position as a tenured Professor of Forensics at Georgetown. Emmie viewed her team as a rare example of the perfect synchrony of diversities coming together to create an ideal result.

"So what's going on, guys?" Emmie asked as she slid onto the chair at the head of the table. Looking up from the pile of papers in front of her, Sarah replied, "Oh, it's a bad one Boss. A real bad one. Three bodies found, female, mutilated and sexually assaulted near Charlottesville." Taking the folder Sarah handed her, Emmie opened it to the forensic photographs and reports inside. All three of the young women had been beaten savagely and were covered in massive bruising and lacerations. There were ligature marks on all, and each victim had one limb missing. They were naked and positioned in a sexually suggestive manner. Despite having worked on many cases such as this one in the past, Emmie still experienced an adrenaline-fueled charge when she was faced with a new challenge. She looked up at her team, gauging their reactions. Raj spoke first, "Emmie, I know this may sound a little far-fetched, but the markings and the killing style looks to me as an exact replica of the killings committed by The Darwin Killer in London." Startled, Emmie let out a slight gasp and widened her eyes. "Raj, you are talking about killings that took place some thirty years ago!" She replied. Seeing the other team members' confused expressions, Emmie took a deep breath and launched into an explanation. "The murders that Raj is talking about took place about three decades ago in a very seedy part of Soho in London. Numerous dark-haired, rather exotic-looking women, between the ages of twenty-one and thirty, were found mutilated, semi dismembered and left in suggestive poses for someone to find. Because some similar murders were found in a few other European countries, both local police and Interpol were involved. A few years later, the same style of killings was showing up here. I will let Raj give you more details, he was on the front line during this." Raj scanned the room, and began, "Well I was a rookie at the time this was happening and thrilled to be involved. The first time I was at a crime scene and saw the victim, I was very concerned that I was going to lose my lunch and be the laughing stock of Interpol. But I held it together, THAT time." After a dry chuckle and shake of his head, he continued, "The murders kept piling up, all women who had the same look. They all had marks from being restrained. They all had been sexually assaulted. Most had a limb missing, and all were placed as though they were posing for a sexy picture. By the time the killer finally made a mistake and we got him, we had twenty-four KNOWN bodies. We all knew that there were more, but we could never get him to give us any clues. So there are probably victims we will never find. Since England does not have a death sentence, this monster will just rot in jail until he dies in his sleep or one of the other inmates shank him." As Raj paused to catch his breath before continuing, Kaitlyn interrupted with "Wait a minute. You said you caught this dude, it was like 30 years ago, and he is still incarcerated. So how does this pertain to our current case? And why is he called the Darwin Killer?" Raj smiled indulgently and continued with his narrative: "He is called the Darwin Killer because he repeatedly told us when we were interrogating him that the women's deaths were justified because it was 'survival of the fittest.' His real name is Jonathan Wright, and he was from Liverpool, but then moved here. And the reason this seems crucial to me is because of the blatant similarities to this case in front of us now." As Shawn and Robert both tried to interject, Emmie raised her hand for silence. "OK, guys, enough for now. We have a two-hour drive ahead of us to discuss this further. Everyone make whatever arrangements you need to, and we will meet back here in thirty minutes. We are headed to Charlottesville."

Chapter 2

Emmie pulled up in front of the Charlottesville Police Station in her government-provided SUV, accompanied by Sarah and Shawn. Raj, Kaitlyn and Robert pulled in behind her. With Emmie in lead, the team walked briskly up the walk and through the glass doors. Upon entering, they were met by a distinguished-looking man, who introduced himself as Captain Whitaker. He ushered them toward the back of the building, where he directed them into a large conference room. "I hope this will be adequate for you to set up in," he said. Emmie smiled and nodded her approval, and after giving a brief introduction of her team, asked, "Do you have time to give us a summary of what you have discovered so far?" The Captain gestured for her and the others to sit, and began to speak…"I called you in not just because of the murders but also because of some additional concerns. These three women were all around the same age, all had long dark hair, had a degree of exotic ethnicity, were petite in size, were sexually assaulted, and their bodies were all positioned in a similar way. In addition, over the last week, there have been four missing person reports, involving young women matching the same description. There is definitely some sort of pattern, and I am afraid we are in over our heads here." Captain Whitaker cleared his throat, and with a visible flush, added, "To be honest Dr. Blanchet, they look an awful lot like you!"

After settling the flurry of excitement that the Captain's last remark sparked in her team members and herself, Emmie regained control and began assigning duties to her group. "Sarah, I want you to get online and do a comprehensive search of all missing persons matching the description of our victims. Start with this general area, but then expand the search to include nationwide reports. Raj, I would like you to do the same, but focus on International records, primarily Great Britain. Shawn and Kaitlyn, I would like you to get the addresses of the families of the victims and the missing girls, and go to their homes to interview them. Focus on common denominators. Robert, I would like you to come with me to the morgue to talk to the medical examiner. Keep in touch, and we will meet back here in a few hours."

After her team dispersed, and after leaving a request with the police captain to notify her of any new developments, Emmie and Robert set out to the morgue to meet with the M.E. Since the morgue was only a couple of blocks away, they decided it was easier to walk. While en route, Robert looked at Emmie and inquired, "How do you feel about what Whitaker said? That all the victims look like you?"

Emmie tossed her hair back impatiently, saying, "Oh that's so ridiculous! Because they have dark hair and are petite? There are millions of women who match that description! I think he is just grasping at straws right now, he needs this case solved. Let's just focus on the facts at hand." Robert wisely fell silent and walked beside her without further comment.

The distinctive odor of disinfectant and death assaulted their nostrils as they walked into the morgue. Robert immediately reached into his pocket for the little jar of Vicks that he carried with him for these odorous occasions. Emmie shook her head in refusal as he offered some to her, saying, "No thanks, it doesn't bother me." She was grateful for her ability to blot out external stimuli while focusing on a case. She didn't need any distractions right now. A gray-haired man, along with his younger assistant was busy working on one of the bodies. He looked up as they walked toward him, and with a pleasant smile said, "Hi, I am Doctor Johannson, but just call me Al. I am guessing you are the FBI?"

"Yes, we are. I am Dr. Blanchet and this is Dr. Montgomery, but feel free to call us Emmie and Robert. What have you learned so far about the victims?"

"Well," the friendly medical examiner replied, "all three victims had identical wounds, they ranged in age from twenty-three to twenty-seven, all had dark hair and eyes, and were all around five feet tall in height. They all had ligature marks around their necks and wrists, one also had similar marks on her ankles." Walking closer to the tables where the three bodies lie, he continued, "this victim here had dismemberment of her left arm, this one here had her left leg amputated, and this poor lass lost both of her arms. Tox screens for all three were negative. COD for all three was exsanguination. Two of them had tearing and abrasions suggesting sexual assault."

"Do you have a time of death?" asked Emmie.

"Within the last 24 hours," Al replied.

Trying to hide her impatience, Emmie asked, "No, I mean for each victim. What was the time of death for each girl?"

With a grimace, the M.E. blurted, "This is what I am trying to tell you. All three appear to have died within a few minutes of one another!"

Chapter 3

After leaving the morgue and returning to the police station, Emmie and Robert were joined by Sarah and Raj, who had stayed at the station to conduct research and searches. Sarah appeared excited and eager to share her findings. "Wait one moment," Emmie pleaded, "I need coffee." A few minutes later, with a steaming mug in hand, she settled into a chair and gestured for them to begin.

Sarah spoke up first, "Ok. I first searched the city of Charlottesville, then I widened my parameters to the neighboring areas of Harrisonburg and Fredericksburg. Then I widened them even further to Virginia Beach, and then all the way to Bristol. I eventually looked into the entire east coast. I started looking over a time period of five years, and then broadened that to twenty years." Knowing that Sarah had a flair for the dramatic and had a slight tendency to showboat, Emmie did her best to wait patiently for her to continue. "I found twenty-three women who meet the criteria, with eight being between the years 2000 and 2008, and the remainder being in the last four years. Of that twenty-three, twelve bodies were actually found, displayed in the manner of the latest victims. The found bodies were also in the last four years. These cases are all classified as unsolved."

"Good work Sarah," praised Emmie, then turned to Raj expectantly.

"Well Boss, you are not going to be happy. I not only searched Great Britain but I changed my parameters to include most of Europe. After the arrest of the Darwin Killer, there were no significant findings in our search range." Nodding with understanding, Emmie assured Raj that was what she had expected and she knew how thorough he was.

A few moments later, Shawn and Kaitlyn returned. They appeared frustrated with the results of their interviews, revealing that while most of the families they met with were cooperative, they were unable to gather any information which lent itself to a correlation between the victims. They were unable to find a common ground of any sort. "Well," sighed Emmie, "we will need to keep looking. There has to be a link, there has to be."

Kaitlyn hesitated for a moment, then suggested, "Is it possible that the only link is their physical appearance?"

"It is definitely a possibility." Emmie replied, "And one we need to stay on top of."

Shawn nodded in agreement, "We checked interests, careers, friends, places they shopped, places they hung out, internet interests, clubs…whatever. No similarities at all."

"Ok," Emmie replied, "you guys know I have all the faith in the world in you, so I trust your findings. But I just feel in my gut that there is something we are missing. Maybe…" Before she could finish, Captain Whitaker burst into the room.

"We have another body. Same MO. This time she was found at the Shenondoah National Park a few miles away."

Chapter 4

Shenandoah National Park encompasses part of the Blue Ridge Mountains in the Commonwealth of Virginia. The park is long and narrow, with the Shenandoah River and its broad valley to the west, and the rolling hills of the Virginia Piedmont to the east. Emmie, her crew, and Captain Whitaker rode on the main park road, Skyline Drive, to reach their destination. They had been traveling for some time when around a bend they came upon a group of official vehicles with flashing red and blue lights. "Oh great," mumbled Whitaker, "now the Forest Service has their fingers in the pot as well. Just what we need." Emmie pulled the SUV she was driving over to the side, and the vehicles behind her followed suit. She marched purposefully toward the officers standing there and introduced herself. One of the men came forward, his six feet height towering over Emmie's petite five feet frame. With a friendly face, he presented himself as the officer in charge, Supervisory Forest Ranger Joel McNeil. Emmie offered her hand and it seemed to disappear in McNeil's strong grasp. He was fully prepared to be candid about his displeasure about what he perceived as interference from the FBI, but once he gazed upon Emmie's flawless beauty, he felt helpless. Staring at her dumbly, it was Emmie that finally broke the silence. "What have your men found?" she asked.

McNeil gathered his wits and replied, "The body was found just a few hundred feet into the woods, I can fill you in as we walk." Emmie nodded her agreement, gestured to her team to follow, and the group trudged up the trail. As they walked, McNeil gave her the details of the findings, as promised. She returned the courtesy by sharing what information she had about the other dead women.

Reaching such enviable accomplishments at such a young age was the result of hard work and very little focus on romance or dalliances for Emmie. She dated seldom, and they were casual dinner dates generally and never developed beyond one or two meetings. It was her experience that men outside of her profession were intimidated by her line of work, and men within the field were envious of her achievements. But as McNeil was talking, she found herself staring at his intensely blue eyes, his rugged profile, and his strong arms generating an unfamiliar rush of warm feelings. Giving herself a mental reproach, she forced herself to tear her eyes away and gaze at her surroundings. She needed to remember that although the forest was lush with teeming life, that just around the bend death had made its presence known..

As they approached the site of the crime, the group saw a dozen or more officers and forensic techs gathered around a form lying on the ground. Drawing nearer, she saw the naked body of a young, slightly built, dark-haired woman. The body had multiple stab wounds, and her right hand had been amputated. She was suggestively posed spread eagle. Shawn, standing at her side, mumbled "Just like all the others." Emmie nodded grimly in agreement and squatted down to get a closer look. As she looked up, she noticed the familiar face of Al, the Medical Examiner. As they made eye contact, he shook his head bleakly at the sight before them. Drawing closer, he remarked, "Well, it sure looks like the identical M.O. as the other victims, I will know for sure when I get her back to the morgue. I hope this bastard gets caught soon before he does this to more innocent young women."

"Don't we all!!" Emmie replied.

Upon leaving the park, Emmie and Whitaker headed to the Morgue, with the rest of the team tackling various duties as assigned. The unpleasant odors assaulted their nostrils as they walked in. Dr. Johanson, or "Al" as he preferred to be called, was apparently still at the crime scene, but his assistant looked up as they walked in. An unremarkable appearing man, both in physical appearance and manner, he stared blankly at them as they entered. Emmie reminded him of who they were, but the man simply grunted and mumbled something under his breath. Without the latest victim there, it didn't seem worthwhile for them to stay, so they asked the less than friendly assistant to have Al call them when he had the final results. As they walked back out into the fresh air, Whitaker informed Emmie that he had a few errands to run and would meet her back at the station. She agreed to meet him there. As she slid behind the wheel of her SUV, her phone rang. Without looking, she grabbed and answered, "Dr. Blanchet, FBI." There was a soft chuckle on the other end, then a male voice replied, "Bonjour Docteur Blanchet. C'est Docteur Blanchet. Ton père." (Hello Dr. Blanchet. This is Doctor Blanchet. Your father.) "We need to discuss this interest of yours in the Darwin Killer case."

"Pere! Que faistu?" She asked lovingly. Emmie's favorite person was her father and was the one who inspired her to follow the career path she had chosen. Although their careers often frequently made contact difficult, they both made efforts to keep in touch as much as life would allow. "How did you know I was following the case?" she asked.

"I have my resources," he chuckled, "you know I keep an eye on you!" Emmie settled back against the seat and summarized what she knew so far about the murders, and how they seemed to do mimic the MO of The Darwin Killer. André listened quietly until she finished. "Ma cherie, you do realize that Wright committed these murders before you were even born, and he is languishing in prison as we speak."

"I do know that, Dad, but surely you can see the common factors here!" she exclaimed.

"I do," he replied, "and that is what concerns me. We obviously have some sort of copycat, perhaps someone who studied Wright's crimes. Let me do some searching, and I will get back to you. By the way, it is your Mother's birthday Saturday, and we are going to Le Maison to celebrate. Can you join us?" Emmie assured him that she would do her best, and after a few pleasantries, ended the conversation.

Chapter 5

After grabbing a quick bite to eat, Emmie headed back to the police station. Once she greeted her colleagues and Captain Whitaker, she pulled out her laptop and began scouring through the archives. Although she was afraid that she had already accessed all the data available on the Darwin Killer, she hoping to find something she may have previously overlooked. She browsed for an hour or so and was feeling her eyes burn with fatigue. Suddenly, she sat upright in her chair, and yelled, "Raj, come here! You need to see this!" As he came to her, she pointed to her screen and said, "This is the one that I haven't seen before." The article she was referring to, included the information they had seen numerous times, such as the names of the victims, the general circumstances, the descriptions, as well as the usual theories. However, this site provided additional information that none of them had previously read. The article revealed that during the arrest, Wright's wife had tried to protect her husband, and aimed a pistol at the arresting officers. This resulted in the police firing a fatal shot that subsequently killed her, leaving the Wrights' six-year-old son a witness and an orphan. The child had no close relatives, and thus became a ward of the state and spent his life in several foster homes before reaching adulthood. He hadn't been heard from since he turned 18. Barely unable to contain her excitement, she looked up at Raj and asked, "This is an interesting development, don't you think?" Her enthusiasm was cut short at the look of intensity on his face. "What's wrong my friend?" she asked. Instead of answering, he leaned over to scroll a bit further down the page, then gestured to the next paragraph. What she read next made her gasp with shock. The article stated that the officer who fired the fatal shot was rookie Interpol agent André Blanchet.

"Did you know about this? You worked with him!" she inquired. Raj shrugged and looked physically ill.

He replied sheepishly, "yea I did. But it happened before you were even born, and I assumed he would have told you when you were old enough to understand. This haunted him something fiercely for a long time."

"That's probably why he was so interested when I started looking into that old case. He was afraid I was going to find out. Why would he hide this from me?"

"Go easy on him, he was probably trying to protect you. You know, and everyone knows, that you are his world. Why don't you just talk to him?"

With a hiss, she replied, "Oh I plan on it!"

After André retired from Interpol ten years ago, and after a few years working in Homeland Security, he and his wife Chloe moved to Alexandria. André now ran a private security company, while Chloe still toured sometimes, and taught music at the university part-time. While Emmie loved her mother, she did not have the bond with her that she enjoyed with her father. Chloe had an aloof manner that often made her appear unapproachable. Combined with a very critical eye for perfection, she often did not exude warmth or welcoming maternal vibes. Emmie adored her father, as much as he adored her. She also was very close to her maternal grandparents, who had acted as caregivers throughout much of Emmie's childhood, due to her parents' demanding careers. Throughout Emmie's life, Chloe sometimes appeared to harbor some resentment and perhaps jealousy regarding this closeness that Emmie had with her other family members. This often resulted in Emmie feeling even more alienated from her mother.

Pulling into the parking lot of the Security Company her father owned, Emmie did a brief mental rehearsal of what she wanted to say to him. She mulled over possible reasons that he withheld this from her while she worked very hard at not losing her temper at her favorite person. As she walked into the building, the reception area guard recognized her and waved her through. She stepped into the elevator and pushed the button for the third floor. When the door opened, she stepped out and immediately saw her father standing nearby talking to one of his employees. Almost simultaneously, he saw her and broke into a wide grin. However, when he looked into her face his smile disappeared and he said, "Let's go into my office." Once inside, he turned to her expectantly. "Ok, ma cherie. I know that face. What is up?"

Emmie sat down and looked at her father searchingly. "Is there anything you want to tell me about the Darwin Killer case?" she asked.

André, visibly flushed, stood up without answering and walked over to his coffee maker. He offered her a cup, but she impatiently shook her head in refusal. Her foot was beating an irritated tap on the floor while she waited for him to finish his task and sit. When that finally happened, she repeated her question. "I feel you already know the answer to that, or you wouldn't be asking me that," he replied.

"Yea I do, but I want to hear it from you," she replied. "Why didn't you tell me? What really happened? I thought we always were so open with one another!! I just want to understand."

He took a swallow of his coffee, let out an audible sigh, and said, "Yes, I do always tell you everything. I had my reasons for keeping this from you."

"Well I would like to hear those reasons now," she replied. Gazing intently at his daughter, André nodded, cleared his throat, and began to speak.

Chapter 6

"The Darwin Killer case was, for the most part, my first major case after joining Interpol. I had only been with the agency for a little over a year, and the bulk of my exposure had been dealing with international thieves and con men. Being assigned to this highly publicized crime pretty much was the catalyst that advanced my career. When Wright was finally apprehended in his home, everyone's adrenaline was sky-high. I have looked back at that day hundreds of times, wondering if I was being overly zealous, or impulsive. But each time, I come to the same conclusion. There was simply no other choice. She aimed a gun at me and did not respond to instructions to lay it down."

Emmie nodded somewhat impatiently, "Yes I am sure it was your only option. I know about the shooting…I read all of this. What I need to know is why I had to read about this in an old article clipping rather than hearing it from you?"

André looked away, and after what seemed like an eternity he replied, "I was protecting you."

"From what?" she exclaimed, "I am a professional too, I can take care of myself!" Without replying, he stood up and walked over to a locked file cabinet, and pulled out a large folder. Taking it back to his seat, he shuffled through until he reached the paper he was looking for. Silently, he handed it to his daughter, and sat back, studying her face as she read. The police file listed numerous incidents in which Wright had boasted that he would seek revenge on André for the death of his wife, and insisted that he had the resources to enforce this. Further down the page, Emmie's eyes focused on a statement that the prisoner had made, a statement that he made just a little over two years ago, that read "Blanchet feels so safe in his high-security castle, so untouchable. But I have ways to hurt him without coming anywhere near him. He took my family, I will take his. He will know my pain when he loses those whom he loves. I will find a way, and he won't see it coming. This is my promise to my dear wife."

Emmie raised her eyes to meet her father's, and said softly, "Dad, I get it. But don't you think that I should have known this, to be aware of the threats?"

"Maybe," he replied, "But I wanted to make sure you didn't worry. I am taking care of this. I have people watching him from inside the prison. He isn't going to hurt you ma chère. Please don't be mad at me." She shook her head slowly and with a grin assured him she never could stay angry at him, for too long. After receiving reassurance that he was not withholding anything else, she left to head back to the station.

Once she was reunited with her team, Emmie immediately updated them about the visit with her dad and what she found out. When she finished, she reassured them that she was not concerned, and they needed to focus their attention on the case. She asked if Al had contacted any of them with the autopsy results from the latest victim. After receiving a negative reply from all, she decided to place a call to him. He answered after the first ring. They exchanged some brief pleasantries and then asked if there were any new discoveries. "No, unfortunately," he replied. "It is exactly the same as the other victims. So frustrating! I have been waiting to hear from you though, I was wondering if there was anything new at your end." Puzzled, she answered, "No, but I have been waiting to hear from YOU. I left a message with your assistant."

Al sighed, "Oh Brian. Yea, he sure is an odd one. He seldom talks, and is about as friendly as a rock. But he works his ass off for me, never takes a sick day, and is always on time. I guess I can't have it all," he chuckled. They shared a laugh and ended the call.

She had no sooner placed her phone on her desk when it rang. Looking down, she did not recognize the number. "Hello, Dr. Blanchet," she answered.

"Hi, this is Joel McNeil, from the Forest Service. We met at the crime scene earlier, do you remember me?" He asked. Emmie felt a flush across her cheeks and over her whole body. It had been a very long time since she experienced such a visceral reaction from any man, just from hearing his voice. Forcing herself to stay calm and professional, she assured him that she did indeed remember him. What he said next snapped her fully into attention. "We have another victim in the park." Emmie assured him that she would gather her team and be there as soon as possible. As she hung up, she saw her entire crew staring at her.

"More bad news Boss?" asked Kaitlyn.

"Yup," she replied. "Gather your gear, we are heading back into the woods."

When they arrived at the National Park, the Forest Service vehicles were lined up at the trailhead entrance. Joel immediately saw Emmie and her team, and briskly walked over to them. "Is this the same as the others?" she asked.

Joel nodded grimly, "exactly." They walked silently together down the trail just a few yards before they reached the crime scene. The victim placement was identical to the other victims. Shaking her head in frustration, Emmie turned away but paused when something glossy a few yards away caught her eye. Gesturing to Joel, they walked together to investigate. As she stepped over a tree root, her foot caught it and she started to lose her balance. When Joel grabbed her waist to steady her, he did not immediately let go. As they gazed into one another's eyes, Emmie knew instantly that the strong feelings of attraction were mutual. For a moment, time stood still until they both heard the rustling of footsteps headed their way. Snapping back into focus, they walked the additional few steps to see what had caught their attention. Piled against a tree was a stack of photos. Joel picked them up with a gloved hand, and his face immediately paled. "What is it?" Emmie asked. When he didn't reply, she insisted he hand them over to her. With obvious reluctance, he handed her the stack. She recoiled as she looked at dozens of photographs of herself. Some were taken outside her office, while others showed her at her favorite coffee shop, at the store, even at the park. Visibly shaken, but with resolve, she uttered, "Well this proves what I have suspected all along. It is ME who is the main target here. I need to process this." After promising to keep Joel up to date on any findings, she headed back to her team.

Chapter 7

Emmie called and updated her father as she drove back to the office. That conversation did not go well, with André insisting that she drop out of the case, and go into protective custody, while Emmie rebutting that she was a trained agent and knew how to protect herself. André went as far as threatening to call the FBI Director and asking that she be removed from the case, with Emmie stopping short of informing him that he was retired and no longer had any influence. The exchange ended with Emmie agreeing curtly to be extra vigilant and to always have other agents with her. Her head was pounding as she hung up. She hated disagreeing with her beloved parent, but sometimes he needed to be reminded she was no longer a child and was indeed an accomplished professional.

When she arrived at the office, her team was waiting for her. On the drive, she had instructed Sarah to gather the others and to ask everyone to continue with paper and electronic searches for any clues that they may have overlooked. Grabbing a quick coffee, she settled in, staring at the blank computer screen as her mind raced. "I now know for sure that this is about me," she considered. "But how am I involved? Is it because of Dad? They are watching

my every move! It has to be someone I know. But who?"
Her musings were cut short by a text alert. Recognizing the
number as belonging to Joel McNeil, she swiped to open the
message. What she read, put a smile on her face. "Hi. I know
this is a crazy time, and this case takes everyone's full
attention. Maybe I am nuts, but I felt like we had a moment
out there earlier. Was it just me? I would like to explore this
and see where it goes. After this mess is over, would you
meet me for a drink?"

She took a moment to respond, and then texted back:
"No it wasn't just you. But you are right, this case has my
full focus. Ask me again when it is over." She followed the
text with a smiley face and hit send. Ten seconds later he
responded with a thumbs up. Settling back to attention on
the case, she grimaced when her phone again beeped. "I
sure hope he isn't going to be overly persistent," she
thought. But as she opened the text, it was from a different
sender, and the message read, "This is Doctor Johannson.
Come to the lab ASAP. I have information for you."

"Wow, that seemed rather curt. Whatever happened to
him wanting to be called Al," she thought with a shrug.

After informing her team where she was going, she left
to meet him. Although it was getting dark, it was pleasant
out, so again she decided to walk the few blocks to the
morgue. Entering the building, she strode with purpose
down the long hallway to the lab. The lights were on but the
lab appeared empty when Emmie walked in. "Hello," she
called. "Is anyone here?"

"Looks like most of the employees have gone for the
day," she thought. Her phone started ringing persistently,
and seeing that it was Joel she answered with, "Hi Joel, this

is not a good time. Can I call you back?" His tone of voice was so urgent and pressured that she could hardly recognize it. "Emmie, listen to me, you need to get out of there NOW. I am headed your way. Just get the hell out of there!"

"Wow, what on earth was that about?" she puzzled. Placing her phone back into her pocket and turning to leave, she suddenly felt a stabbing pain in the side of her neck. The world then faded away into darkness.

Chapter 8

Emmie awoke to sensations of being hung over, complete
with nausea and headache. She was aware of discomfort in
her back, the feeling of lying on something hard. Taking in
her surroundings, she recognized that she was lying in a
forest, and the sun was just beginning to rise. Emmie
struggled to sit up, which was difficult since her hands were
tied behind her back. Fighting back the waves of nausea and
dizziness, she tried to calm her pounding heart and regain
some sort of rational thought. "I have been drugged," she
realized. The restraints on her wrists seemed rather loose,
and with some twisting, she was able to squeeze her small
hands out of the rope. Standing up brought another wave of
vertigo, but she brushed it off as she looked around to assess
her situation. Emmie identified her surroundings as the
National Park, very close to where the victims had been
found. She realized that her bag, along with her gun, was
missing. However, her phone was still in her pocket, where
she had placed it after her last conversation with Joel.
Pulling it out of her pocket, she checked for a signal. "Of
course there isn't a signal. This is like a freaking horror
movie," she thought and chuckled grimly at the irony.
Hoping that there was enough signal for texting, she quickly

typed "SOS. I have been abducted and taken to the crime scenes." As she hit send, she heard a rustle of leaves, and her phone was yanked out of her hand as she was shoved roughly to the ground. Staring down at her, was Brian, Dr. Johannson's assistant.

Stunned momentarily, she gaped at the menacing man hovering over her, with a gun pointed at her face. His face was devoid of any expression, except for his eyes. They were teeming with cold hatred and pure evil. "Who are you?" she asked. He remained silent for what seemed like an eternity, and when he spoke it was in a flat tone, without any perceivable effect.

"I have waited for this moment most of my life," he began. "I have waited, and watched, and planned. I knew my day would come when I could achieve my goal. It took all my strength not to come to you too soon. That would have ruined everything. So I waited as patiently as I could, I knew I would get my chance. When the urge for revenge would become too strong, I would choose a surrogate, a look-alike, for temporary relief. They were like a Band-Aid for me until I could finally have the real thing."

Stunned, Emmie retorted, "What the hell? You are killing innocent girls because they look like me?"

The madman shook his head impatiently, "Damn...they were just collateral damage. They didn't matter!"

"Why?" she asked. "I don't even know you! What in the world do you think I ever did to you?"

Quietly he replied, "You were born the daughter of André Blanchet."

Emmie tried to control her breathing as she responded to her attacker. "Yes, I am. What problems do you have with my father?"

He gazed at her coldly and replied, "He killed my mother." Aghast with what she just heard, Emmie stared at her attacker wordlessly. After she gathered her senses, she asked, "Just who ARE you?"

With a grin full of malice, the man replied, "I am Brian Wright. My father is Jonathan Wright, who has been suffering in prison for over thirty years. My sweet wonderful mother was Elizabeth Wright, sweet and wonderful until your father took her life as she tried to protect her family. I have watched you for years. I was tossed from foster home to foster home, beaten and even worse things were done to me, so many times over the years. As I grew older I started researching about the perfect Agent André Blanchet, and I followed everything I could about his career and personal life. After you were born, it became very apparent that his world revolved around you, just the way mine revolved around my mother. I realized then that the best way to get my vengeance is to take away the thing he loves most."

"But you are talking about murder. Many murders. He didn't murder your mother. He was following police protocol. She pulled a gun on him and didn't respond to demands to comply with laying down the weapon. He was just doing his job!" she cried. His face blackened with fury as he rushed toward her, and yanked her to her feet, slamming her against the nearby large pine tree. Gasping with shock and pain, she struggled to regain her breath, as he lifted her by the throat and held her against the tree.

"You bitch," he spat, "You didn't know my mother. You have no right to talk about her. You don't know a damn thing, you were not there. I was, and I have remembered it every day of my life."

Just as Emmie started to feel consciousness leave her, he released his grip on her and she slid back to the standing position against the tree. Fighting to regain some rational thoughts, she attempted to keep her voice calm as she asked, "You have kidnapped and killed innocent women, but you have stalked and watched me for years? Why am I still alive?"

Giving her a hideously vile grin, he replied, "Oh I am taking my time with you. Your father will have the image of your mutilated ravaged body forever imprinted on his brain."

"I have to think of something to buy some time here," she thought. She put her hands out toward him in a beseeching manner, "I can only imagine how awful it had to have been, seeing your mother shot in front of your eyes. But do you think she would have wanted you to do these things? To hurt innocent people like this?"

"Innocent?" he snarled at her. As they were talking, she saw some movement in the woods about twenty yards behind him. It was a fat, happy-looking squirrel, innocently jumping from one low hanging branch to the next. Suddenly, the little creature knocked a small limb free, and it fell to the ground with a racket. Wright was startled and turned quickly to look, and Emmie, thinking quickly, seized the opportunity to grab the closest big stick and strike him in the back of the head. Without looking back, she began running through the forest.

Chapter 9

Emmie had been running for what seemed like an eternity. Her lungs felt like they were on fire, and her legs were shaky, making her feel off balance. But she knew her survival depended on her being able to keep on moving. "I can't go much longer," she thought. "But dammit, I am not going to let him win. I am stronger than this." Pushing with everything she had, she rounded a bend in the trail and saw a small cave in an overhead ledge. Scaling the shelf, she crawled inside the diminutive opening and collapsed. Twisting around she realized she could see outside, but due to the angle of the entrance and the height of the ledge, it would be next to impossible for anyone to spot her. Shaking uncontrollably, she hid there, trying to regain normal breathing. Suddenly, she heard rustling and heavy breathing. Peeking out, she saw Wright lumbering up the trail, soaked in sweat. He was a bulky man and lacked the grace and flexibility that Emmie's petite body possessed. He stopped to lean against a large boulder to catch his breath, looking around as he did. Emmie froze, trying to keep her respirations as silent as possible. "Oh no! He is not leaving!" Wright plopped onto the ground with a big sigh, his chest heaving with exertion, his head oozing blood from where he had been hit with the stick. "He definitely seems to be in worse shape than me," she thought. As she watched, Wright appeared to be falling into a sleep state. She waited until his breathing slowed down into what appeared to be a dozing pattern, and she decided it was now or never. Stealthily crawling forward, with her eyes never leaving her predator, she inched toward the edge of the ledge. She was almost there when suddenly a large bird landed on the ledge beside her. Emmie tried to silently shoo it away, but it stared at her blankly. As she became more aggressive with her hand gestures, the bird retaliated with a loud squawk and then flew away. Unluckily, the sound aroused Wright, who with a grunt, lumbered to his feet and the two locked eyes. Pulling his pistol from his pocket, he started to climb toward her. When she scampered behind a substantial-sized boulder, he began firing shots. Emmie felt a searing pain as one of the shots grazed her upper arm. He was getting closer and closer. "I am not going out like this," she contemplated. "I am better than him. That bastard is not going to get me!" With every bit of strength in her slight body, she shoved as hard as she could against the boulder. At first, it refused to budge. Filled with desperation, she took a deep breath and pushed as hard as she could. The rock suddenly broke free and rapidly rolled off the ledge. With a sickening crunch, the boulder landed on top of her pursuer. He lay there silently. Grimacing in pain and bleeding profusely from her arm wound, she cautiously descended from her perch and walked over to where Wright was lying. With one glance it was obvious that he was never going to get back up. Half delirious with pain, fatigue and the aftereffects of whatever he had drugged her with, she started to walk up the trail toward what she hoped was the parking lot entrance.

Although Emmie had wrapped her light jacket around her injured arm as a makeshift bandage, the blood had soaked through and was starting to drip down her side. Her legs felt encased with cement with every step that she took, and her vision was blurring. "I can't die out here, I have to keep going." Just when she felt that she couldn't take another step, she saw the entrance and parking lot in the distance. Relief flooded her and she forced herself forward. "Just a few more steps, just a few more," she silently urged herself. As she drew closer, the spinning in her head increased and her knees buckled and she fell to the ground. Random thoughts raced through her head, "I smashed that son of bitch with a rock just like Road Runner does to Wile E Coyote. Does Dad know I am here? Does anyone know I am here? Am I going to die?" As her mind grew foggier, she heard the sound of car doors slamming and people calling her name. Then blackness overtook her.

Chapter 10

When Emmie opened her eyes, she was in strange surroundings. She realized she was in a hospital, and her father was sitting next to her bed. His voice was fraught with emotion as he spoke, "Oh ma fille chérie. Vous êtes réveillés!"

Emmie chuckled softly, "You must have been worried. You always forget your English when you are under stress."

André kissed her forehead, "Oh you don't know!! I was sick with worry. Your poor mother was beside herself. She just left to get some rest, as did your team. The whole bunch was here all night. How do you feel? You lost a lot of blood."

After squirming around in her bed, she answered him with a laugh, "Well I sure feel better knowing that monster is dead!"

"Oui, ma chère, he is gone. You took care of that."

"Have all the bodies been found?" she asked.

André shrugged grimly, "We can only hope."

When her father left to get her something to drink, Emmie took a moment to reflect on the events of the last few days. She was stunned by the fact that someone had been stalking her for years, and she was completely oblivious to it. She had always prided herself on being super vigilant and aware of her surroundings. When Andrés returned with her soft drink, he told her that she had a visitor waiting to see her. "Who is it?" she asked.

"It is a very nice gentleman who has been here since you were brought in. He has been very worried about you. May I allow him to come in?" he asked. Emmie nodded her agreement, and André walked out of the room. A few seconds later she heard a movement and looked up to see Joel smiling down at her.

"Well look who's awake," he said with a tired grin. "You look wonderful," he added.

Gazing up at him, she felt tears welling in her eyes. Angry at herself, she rubbed at them impatiently, "I don't know why I am getting so emotional all of the sudden," she mumbled. When she looked up at him, she saw his eyes were glistening too. "I was just afraid that I would never get to take you out for that drink," he blurted throatily.

As he grabbed her hand, she looked up at him, "I wouldn't miss it for the world. Maybe more than one drink? Maybe dinner? Or…whatever?"

He smiled down at her and declared, "You know Darwin was right." When she looked puzzled, he added, "It IS the survival of the fittest, and I will always be grateful for that is what allowed you to get through this. I think we have some interesting developments between us to explore, don't you?"

She looked and him and smiled, "Yes, and I can't wait to see where this will take us!"

Chapter 11

The next day Emmie was released from the hospital with strict instructions to limit her activities for a few days. Although she lost quite a bit of blood from the gunshot wound, the bullet passed clearly through her flesh with minimal damage. The surgeon reassured her that even the scarring would be minimal. Being a bit vain about her appearance, Emmie felt relieved to hear that news!

As she was getting dressed to leave, she heard familiar male voices in the corridor, accompanied by occasional laughter. She smiled as her father, flanked by Joel, entered the room. "Wow," she thought, "These two have become quite the pals. Not sure if that is a good thing or not!"

André quickly strode to her and gave his daughter an affectionate kiss on the forehead. Joel stayed a few steps back and gazed at her with an expression that spoke volumes. Emmie found herself staring at his firm lips and wondering how they would feel planted on her own expectant mouth. Realizing that she was gaping at him, she broke away from her reverie and asked the two men, "What were you guys laughing about out in the hall?"

"Oh, just men stuff," replied her father. "Are you ready to let us spring you from this joint?"

"Oh yes!" Emmie exclaimed eagerly. Just then a nurse entered the room with a wheelchair. "Oh I don't need that," Emmie protested. After insisting that it was hospital policy, the nurse convinced Emmie to allow her to roll her out of the building. Joel and her father followed attentively.

The morning was cloudy and chilly, but even the dreariest weather couldn't dampen Emmie's spirits. The knowledge that the case was solved, she was safe, and she was experiencing romantic feelings she had never felt before gave Emmie a euphoric state of mind that seemed impenetrable. As André went to get the car, Joel waited with Emmie. He leaned toward her and said, "I know you are not up to going out to dinner tonight, and that you need to rest, but I feel selfish. I don't want to wait for our first date. Would it be OK if I picked up some Chinese takeout and brought it over this evening? I mean, I don't want to be pushy, but I just don't want to wait. Besides, you have to eat anyhow!"

Emmie smiled at him, "I don't want to wait either. And yes, that would be great!" As her father drove up with the car, she gave Joel her address and they decided on a time for him to come over. When he grabbed her arm to help her into the car, she felt a thrill course through her body. "This is really happening, and I think it is going to be very interesting," she thought with an inner chuckle.

Chapter 12

After Emmie got home and settled, and after making numerous promises to her father that she would spend the day resting, she headed in to take a nice luxurious hot soak in the tub. As the jets of warm water soothed her sore and tired muscles, she found her thoughts zeroing in on her upcoming evening with Joel. Her emotions ran the gamut from happy anticipation, all the way to nervous apprehension. Was she being foolish for allowing herself to get this emotionally invested in a man? This was such foreign territory for her. Emmie's relationships had always ended poorly, somewhat due to her career obligations as well as her pervasive reluctance to allow herself to become vulnerable. But what she was feeling for Joel was so very different. She wanted to feel that vulnerability, to experience a connection with him. She wanted him to know every part of her. Emmie felt a wave of passion wash over her. "Wow, I do think I am in trouble here," she mused with an inner chuckle.

Joel and Emmie had agreed that he would come over around 7 pm. As the time grew nearer, Emmie's sense of anticipation grew stronger. She busied herself choosing an outfit that would be alluring without looking too contrived, something just right for a casual stay-at-home dinner. She settled for a pair of snug, well-worn jeans that hugged her curves in the right places. She paired them with a red tee with just enough cleavage, and a simple pair of silver earrings. Leaving her long dark hair down, the waves enticingly cascaded over her shoulders. Accompanied by her large brown eyes, pert nose, and lush lips, Emmie was a radiantly beautiful woman. She was well aware of her looks and the effect they had on men. But she chose to instead capitalize on her brain and abilities. While at work, she opted to limit her attire to simple business suits, understated jewelry, and her hair swept up or tied back. In spite of her effects to avoid drawing attention to herself, most people were instantly struck by her perfection to the point of distraction.

Her musings were interrupted by the sound of the doorbell. Emmie's heart raced with excitement. "Calm down girl," she told herself. Taking a deep breath, she walked to the front door and opened it. Joel stood there with a smile on his face, and a large bag of food that emitted tantalizing smells in his hand. His eyes ran over her in an appreciative way without being disrespectful. "You look wonderful, especially for someone who was just shot a couple of days ago," he chuckled. Emmie smiled demurely and invited him in.

The next three hours sped by in what seemed like a heartbeat. The food was delicious, the wine excellent, and the conversation absorbing. Joel and Emmie shared childhood stories, likes and dislikes, interests, and lots of laughter. As they started to clean up after the meal, Joel looked at Emmie and declared, "I can't remember when I have had so much fun!"

Emmie laughed and replied, "And not once did we talk about work! That's a first for me!" Joel laughed in agreement, then fell silent. He continued to gaze at her in a strange and intense way. "What?" she asked.

After a few more seconds he quietly said, "While it is true I have enjoyed every word of what we have talked about this evening, it was a little difficult to focus at times." Emmie looked at him with alarm and asked why. Taking a step closer to her, he looked down into her face and softly said, "Because all night long I found myself staring at your lips and thinking how much I just want to kiss them."

Blushing slightly, Emmie looked into his eyes and replied, "I would like that very much." Without another word Joel swept her into his arms and set her down on the kitchen island. Holding her face in both hands, his lips met hers in a gentle yet passionate kiss. Emmie's head swam with dizziness from the intensity of the feelings. Time seemed to stand still until they finally pulled slightly away and gazed into each other's eyes. Joel broke the silence with a simple "Wow. I mean, WOW!" Giggling like a teenaged girl, Emmie nodded in agreement.

"Yes, this is amazing. But I don't want to rush things. It is too special to mess things up by being in a hurry."

Joel nodded his agreement "We will take as much time as you need, beautiful lady. You are worth waiting for."

Since the next day was a work day for Joel, Emmie walked him to the door, her hand in his. He pulled her toward him to give her one more, sweet lingering kiss. However, this kiss was interrupted by the work ring on

Emmie's phone. Looking down, she saw that the call was from Al. With a hint of annoyance, she thought "Really? What could possibly be so important that couldn't wait until tomorrow?" Gesturing to Joel to wait for a moment, she answered the call. "What's up Al?" The Medical Examiner's voice on the phone was tense, almost frantic.

"Emmie, are you home?" he asked.

Feeling a little impatient, she replied, "Yes, of course. Why?"

After a moment that seemed to be hesitant, Al replied, "Emmie, he's gone. Wright. His body is missing! I went to do his autopsy and his body had vanished! I need to see you right away!"

Chapter 13

Joel insisted on driving Emmie to her visit to the morgue. When they arrived at the building, they found Al appearing very pale and worried. He seemed to relax slightly at the sight of his visitors, but the intense stress was still written on his face. "I don't know what happened," he stammered. "When I opened the drawer to retrieve the body to begin working on it, it simply wasn't there. I checked on him when the body was first brought to me, but I have been inundated with cases the last couple of days, so I just finally had a chance to start my exam. So, I don't know how long the body has been missing. This has never happened to me, not once in my whole career!" Emmie attempted to soothe him while Joel looked around the lab. Uniformed officers were milling around, taking pictures and notes. She observed several of them shooting glances in her direction. As usual, she ignored them and continued with her survey of the surroundings. Nothing looked out of place, no sign of forced entry or damage was apparent anywhere in the building. Suddenly, one of the lab employees approached Al and Emmie and handed his boss a slip of paper. Al's face blanched even more, and he looked at Emmie and Joel with dismay on his face.

"What is it?" Emmie inquired. Wordlessly, Al handed her the folded paper. Curiously she opened it to discover a photocopied picture of herself, with red slashes drawn across her face and nearly illegible handwriting which stated "It's not over yet Bitch!"

The next few minutes were a flurry of activity. Captain Whitaker, who had been in the adjacent room investigating the disappearance, started barking orders at the uniformed officers. Al busied himself with quizzing his staff as to whether they have seen who dropped off the note. Although Emmie was confused and definitely concerned, her training and instinct kicked in and she immersed herself into questioning the staff as well, looking for any clues she could find. Turning to look for Joel, she saw him re-entering the room with his phone in his hand. When she looked quizzically at him, he stated, "I just called my superior. They have been on my back to use my accumulated personal time, and I think this is a very good time to do that. I am officially on leave until further notice."

"But your job! I can't have you…"

Joel cut her off midsentence, "There is no way in HELL that I am letting you out of my sight until this is resolved. Please don't argue with me. My mind is made up." Seeing that Joel's jaw was set with resolve, Emmie nodded her agreement with a secret sense of relief.

When Al came back into the room after questioning his staff, Whitaker lashed out at him, "How could this happen? How can a dead body just get up and walk out?"

Al rubbed his face in frustration, "It can't happen. Dead do not walk. I can only offer one explanation." As Whitaker glared at him impatiently, Al continued. "It is very rare nowadays, but actually was very common as recently as the 19th century. Sometimes, when in a deep unconscious state, their heart rate and respirations get so weak and thread that they can be indiscernible. The paramedics saw the injuries, couldn't find a pulse and declared him deceased. My staff had no reason to check for a pulse when the body arrived, so the body was placed in a drawer waiting for my autopsy."

"Like the horror stories of long ago, about people that would be buried alive, and wake up in a panic and try to dig themselves out of the coffin?" Emmie asked.

"How? How can a severely injured naked man just walk out of here, past security and staff, and not be seen?" Whitaker snapped. Al shook his head in confusion, as Whitaker continued his rant, "Well I will get to the bottom of this, believe me. And heads will roll! No pun intended Doc!"

Chapter 14

Emmie and Joel left the lab a short time later. Joel asked to stop at his condo to grab some clothes and personal items. He had tried to convince Emmie to stay at his place as a safety precaution, but she stubbornly refused. Her compromise was to suggest that he stay in her guest room instead. Joel felt anxious leaving her alone in the car while he packed, so she agreed to come in with him. As they entered his home, Emmie tried to be subtle as she took in her surroundings. As she observed the tasteful but simple décor, she thought, "Wow. This isn't bad, for a man." Everything seemed neat and orderly, without crossing that line of being obsessively so. Emmie blushed when she realized she was trying to sneak a peek into his bedroom. Just then Joel re-entered the living room with a thoughtful and somewhat tense look on his face. But when he looked up and gazed into her face, he seemed to notably relax. "Wow," she thought. "He really is concerned about me! This is a feeling I could sure get used to!"

On the drive to Emmie's house, Joel reached over and held her hand. "There is no way that I will let anything happen to you. I have never felt this was before about anyone, and I have many hopes for the two of us," he murmured. Despite the threat of danger looming around her, Emmie felt a rush of happiness at his touch and words. "I think I am in more trouble with this man and the way I am feeling right now than I am from any serial killer," she humorously mused.

When they arrived at her residence, Emmie was surprised to see two marked police cars sitting on either end of her driveway, and an SUV containing her team sitting in front of the house. By the time she was opening the car door, her crew was out of the vehicle and headed toward her. Raj was leading the group and greeted her with a fatherly hug, exclaiming "Don't worry Em, we have your back. The whole team is working on finding this creep. I promise we will not rest until we know that our fearless leader is safe. Oh, and Whitaker insisted on keeping uniforms at your place 24/7 until this dick is found." Emmie smiled as she forced away tears of gratitude. After giving Raj another quick hug, she walked over to the rest of her team. Struggling to maintain her professionalism, she briefly but efficiently gave them instructions on how to proceed and sent them on their way. Walking back to Joel, her eyes felt moist as she thought, "What a great bunch of people I have looking after me!"

Joel was talking to the uniformed officers and when he saw she had finished with her team, walked over to her. Taking his hand, she thanked him again for what he was doing for her. He smiled at her affectionately and said, "I wouldn't have it any other way, my lady!"

They walked hand in hand into the house and together combed every room checking for anything suspicious. When everything seemed to be in order, Emmie turned to

Joel and said, "I am sorry, but this day has exhausted me. I need to at least try to get some rest. The guest room is over there, there are extra blankets and pillows in the closet if you need them. Help yourself to whatever you want from the kitchen." As she turned away, Joel placed his hand on her shoulder and gently turned her toward him. He stooped down and drew her into his arms. As their lips met, again Emmie felt the world just melt away. Time stood still as their mouths hungrily, yet tenderly sought each other. It was Joel who finally pulled away. "Ok, I will let you get some rest. But please remember I am just a couple of doors away if you need me."

"Oh I need you alright," she thought with a mischievous smile.

In spite of the exhaustion she felt, Emmie was sure that with all the recent events there would little chance of her getting any sleep. However, she dozed off almost immediately and fell into a deep dreamless sleep. It seemed she had barely closed her eyes when she was awakened by the tantalizing smells of bacon cooking and coffee brewing. She stretched sleepily and smiled. "I could so get used to this," she mused. Walking into the kitchen, she was greeted with the sight of Joel at the stove putting together a delicious breakfast. Her heart melted as he turned with a smile and said "Good Morning beautiful. I sure hope you are hungry." The wonderful aromas made Emmie realize that she was famished, and poured herself a steaming cup of coffee.

After devouring the hearty breakfast Joel had prepared, Emmie placed a call to her team. They assured her that along with the FBI, the local and state police were out in force searching for the escaped serial killer. After ending that call, she placed another to her father. She spent several minutes with him trying to convince her to come and stay with him and her mother, and her countering with trying to convince him that she had plenty of protection right where she was. As she finally ended the call, she looked up and saw Joel standing in the doorway. Smiling softly at her, he asked, "Is everything OK with your crew and dad?"

"Yes," she replied, "They are on it. And my dad is being his usual overly protective self. But I think I convinced him I was in good hands." She chuckled.

Joel took a few steps closer to her and began softly massaging her neck. She felt herself leaning into him as he rubbed her tense muscles. "Damn," she mused, "he cooks, he is smart, he is a hottie, he is strong, and he can give neck rubs. Am I dreaming?"

Although Joel was technically off the clock, he had some unfinished paperwork to finish up to make the leave official. Emmie gave him privacy to attack his work, and after checking at the window to see if the officers were still there, busied herself by searching various Federal databases to see what she could find about Wright. After about an hour of searching with little success, she placed a call to her assistant, Sarah. After Emmie outlined what she was looking for, Sarah assured her she would give it her full attention and would call back with any findings.

Emmie wanted to go for a run but realized that in addition to being dangerous, it was too soon after her injury. As she stood up and stretched her arms above her head, she felt a presence behind her and strong arms surround her waist. Joel turned her around slowly, and his eyes spoke louder than words ever could. He drew her against him, and

Emmie could feel the beating of his heart against hers. She marveled at how natural this all felt, this closeness and intimacy. Even though this was all so new for her, it seemed like it was meant to be. "I could stay in his arms forever," she thought. As she gazed up to meet his eyes, he leaned down to place his lips on hers. The moment was shattered by the ring of Emmie's phone. Joel released her with a chuckle, "I guess duty calls!"

The call was from Sarah, informing Emmie that a report containing some very interesting information about Wright had just been sent to her email. Hanging up the phone, Emmie opened her laptop and began to read what Sarah had sent. Joel noticed her sharp intake of breath and stood next to her. "What is it?" he asked.

With wide eyes, Emmie turned to him and replied, "This is worse than we thought. We need to go see my father, now!"

Chapter 15

Joel insisted on driving Emmie to her father's office. On the way over, she gave him an update on her new findings. "Well, the plot thickens with our infamous Mr. Wright. Not only won't the bastard die but he also seems to have been wreaking havoc for longer than we realized." As Joel looked at her quizzically, she continued, "According to the report Sarah sent me, after Wright senior was apprehended and taken into custody, the reports continued of cases of murders with the same MO. These crimes have occurred without interruption throughout the years. Probably more victims than we could ever discover."

With a startled expression, Joel looked at her and said, "Emmie, you do realize that Wright Junior was only six years old when his father was caught?"

She nodded grimly, and in unison, they proclaimed, "accomplice!"

Since Emmie had called her father on the ride to his office, his front desk staff were expecting their arrival and ushered them directly into André's office. After warmly greeting them, André gestured for them to take a seat on the sofa while he took his place behind his desk. Although he appeared warm and cordial, the tension in his face was readily discernible. Emmie wasted no time addressing the subject for the visit. "Père, have you ever suspected there was an accomplice?"

André shook his head vigorously, "No! Never! As far as any of us were concerned, Wright was a one-man show. Nothing ever occurred to draw our attention elsewhere. How did you come to this theory?"

Emmie took a deep breath and began, "Well after the body of Junior disappeared from the morgue, something just didn't feel right to me. I know that Dr. Johannson postulated that Wright wasn't actually deceased but in a coma with a faint pulse, and that may very well be the truth. But to suggest that he just walked out of the building unseen boggled my mind. He was severely injured, I saw the wounds. Hell, I inflicted the wounds! So I asked my tech analyst to do some international searches. What she discovered was that violent murders, matching the exact same pattern as Wright's have continued throughout the last thirty years. There has not been a pause at all, and they continued right after Wright's arrest. Junior was only six at the time. He couldn't have been responsible for the earlier ones!"

"Mais pourquoi n'avons-nous jamais vu cela auparavant?" He inquired. Seeing Joel's puzzled face, André apologized and said in English "But why have we never seen this before?"

Emmie grimaced in frustration, "Probably because no one knew to look! Technology is much more advanced now than it was thirty years ago. These crimes encompassed much of Europe and some of North America. They were so scattered that no one system would have been complex

61

enough to capture all this data. So many different jurisdictions and authorities were involved, many of whom didn't communicate with one another back then. But the technology we have at the Bureau now along with Sarah's genius-level skills, allowed us to see this. So, in addition to finding where Wright took off or was taken off to, we need to find out who this accomplice is." André nodded in agreement and reached for his phone. His hand paused in midair when he saw the look on Joel's face, a look that defied description.

"Mon ami, what is wrong? You haven't said a word during this whole meeting, and now you look like you have seen a ghost. Talk to us!!"

Joel glanced at Emmie, then met André's gaze. "There is something you two aren't considering. We are talking about thirty plus years, and at least two countries. Probably a lot more bodies that never have been discovered or reported. There are how many known victims?"

"The latest count showed about 200 plus," Emmie replied.

Joel looked at her grimly, "and you guys think just two men did that? No freaking way!! I think we may need to consider the possibility that we are looking for a group here. I think this is bigger than we could have ever imagined."

Chapter 16

As Joel drove away from André's office, he glanced at Emmie who appeared deep in thought. "Tell me what you are thinking," he pleaded.

Shaking off her preoccupation, she smiled at him and said, "Sorry, was preparing my instructions for the team so that we can get right on this. I have to admit, it shook me a little when you suggested that there may be a group responsible for these murders. But it makes sense. You were right, there is no way in hell one or two men could be hopping all around the globe doing this. Plus, since this has been happening for more than thirty years, if there was one sole unsub he would be middle-aged or older by now. Chances are he wouldn't be in the physical shape to carry out the extreme violence these killings have been displaying. So it has to be more than one perp. But the question is how many?"

Joel glanced her way and replied, "Let's go back to your place and work on this. But we need to make sure you get some rest too, you are still recuperating you know!"

When they reached Emmie's home, Joel insisted on going in first to do a safety check. She watched him with amusement, thinking, "he does know I am an FBI agent, doesn't he?" When the place met Joel's approval, Joel went to take a shower and Emmie went right to her phone to video chat with her crew. After outlining what she needed from them, and assigning each one a task most suited to their area of expertise, Emmie then ended the video meeting and began her own search. Utilizing various official databases she had access to, she was so intent on her work that she didn't hear Joel come up behind her. The warmth from his skin, fresh from the hot shower, radiated from him as he leaned into her to caress her back. Suddenly, the doorbell rang and startled, she exclaimed, "I am not expecting anyone!"

Joel chuckled softly and said, "Yeah, but I was. Be right back." Emmie heard rustling and voices and then the closing of the door. Curiously she got up from her seat to see Joel carrying bags into the kitchen. He grinned at her mischievously and said, "Hope you don't mind, but I took the liberty to order us some groceries. No offense sweet lady, but your cupboards were as bare as Mother Hubbard's."

Emmie blushed slightly, "Yea, I tend to get a lot of takeouts!" Together, they unpacked his purchases, and then Emmie sat at the island counter as Joel made them thick turkey sandwiches garnished with wedges of fresh fruit. She realized she was famished, and her plate was empty before she realized it. While Joel was cleaning up after their lunch, she found herself gazing at the strong muscles in his back, rippling under his tee. "Wow, that butt is pretty amazing too," she thought and giggled a little without realizing it.

Joel turned around and smiled, "You going to let me in on the joke?"

She smiled and shook her head. "Did you drug me? I feel so sleepy!"

Joel chuckled and admitted, "Yea I feel like I am in a food coma myself." Emmie stood up from the counter to head back to her laptop and found herself a little unsteady on her feet. Joel quickly saw this and sweeping her into his arms like a small child, carried her into the living room, where he laid her onto her sofa. Before she could utter a protest, he gently placed his finger on her lips, "You need to rest. You will be no good to your team, yourself, or this case if you don't take care of yourself. You know I am right!" Too sleepy to object, she drifted off to sleep as Joel placed a pillow under her head and laid a soft blanket over her.

When she again opened her eyes, she realized she had been sleeping for almost two hours. Gazing around the room in an attempt to dispel the blurriness from her eyes, she discovered Joel asleep in the easy chair across the room. His tall frame looked uncomfortably cramped in the chair, and Emmie felt a wave of affection and desire wash over her. As though he could read her mind, he opened his eyes and wordlessly gazed at her for what seemed like a very long time. Silently, he stood up and took a few steps toward the sofa. As she got to her feet and gazed up at him, he silently leaned down and placed his lips on her eagerly awaiting mouth. The kiss seemed endless, and when they finally drew apart, Emmie took him by the hand and led him into her bedroom. Turning to look at him with passion in her eyes, she led him over to her bed. Hoarse with desire, Joel asked, "Are you sure?"

Emmie replied breathlessly, "I have never been more certain of anything in my life," and began to peel off his shirt. Their clothes were quickly and carelessly discarded onto the floor as their hands and lips explored each other's bodies. They fell back on the bed together, limbs entangled. Emmie gave herself to him willingly, and they exploded together in ecstasy.

As they laid in each other's arms, Joel gazed lovingly into her face and said, "I want to tell you something, but I am afraid. I am afraid of scaring you away."

Emmie snuggled even closer, and replied, "I don't think there is anything you could say that would scare me away. So tell me."

Joel pulled back just a little so that he could look directly at her. "I have dated quite a bit. I have slept with women. But I always had a wall up, didn't let myself get too close. I always kept it fun and games. But then I met you. From the first time I laid eyes on you, something has changed. It's like a demolition crew came in and knocked down that wall. I feel things I have never felt before. I have never lost myself in feelings like these, never. It is astonishing, but at the same time terrifying. I feel vulnerable." Silently, Emmie continued to just look at his face. Nervously, Joel pleaded, "Say something. Have I just been weird?"

She smiled and took his face into her small hands. "No it is not weird. Well, yes it is. It is weird because that is exactly how I feel too. I have never felt this close to anyone, nor have I wanted to. So I don't think you could scare me away right now if you tried." Smiling at him impishly, she asked, "Well I have seen how easily you carry me around like I was a baby doll, so I know you are strong. What I would like to know now is, how is your stamina?"

Joel pulled her against him, with laughter in his voice replied. "Well actions speak louder than words, so let me show you!"

Chapter 17

Emmie awoke early the next morning and realized she had a giant smile on her face, and Joel's arm holding her close to him. She could feel his warm breath on the nape of her neck as she basked in this feeling of contentment, unlike anything she had ever experienced before. "I could lie here forever," she mused. As if he could read her thoughts, Joel stirred awake and nuzzled into her hair. As she turned to face him, he opened his eyes and softly kissed her face. "Good morning, beautiful," he sleepily uttered. As Emmie snuggled against his chest, she felt astonished by the pure joy that washed over her. She ran her hands against him, as he kissed her lips passionately.

"I think we need to stop this or we will never get any work done today," she protested.

"Just a couple of minutes, I promise. Just a couple minutes more," he pleaded.

As time flies when lovers are engaged in passion, a couple of minutes became a couple of hours. When Joel and Emmie finally pulled apart, the sun was shining brightly outside the window. Chuckling lightly, Joel said, "Well, I guess brunch would be the appropriate meal now." Emmie suggested that they grab a meal at the coffee house on the way to meet with Captain Whitaker and her father to discuss their new theory. After showering and getting dressed, they headed to Joel's truck. As Emmie looked at him quizzically, Joel explained that he felt that it would be easier to take his vehicle. Since there was no way of knowing how long Emmie had been under surveillance by the possible suspects, it seemed like the less conspicuous option. Nodding in agreement, she climbed into his truck. As he pulled out of her driveway, he glanced at her and asked. "Have you given any more thought to the group perpetrator theory?"

With a sigh, she replied, "Yea. I hate the idea. The whole concept of a cult or gang of violent serial killers is terrifying. But it makes sense. When we look at the whole picture logically, there is no way that just one accomplice could ever be able to pull off all these murders. Especially when we look at the geographical areas that have a history of crimes that match this MO. But I have to confess, I feel a little overwhelmed. Chasing down one killer, even a pair, is hard enough. But a gang with an indeterminate number of participants? Where to even begin!"

Chapter 18

When Joel and Emmie arrived at the police station after brunch, André was already there waiting for them. Greeting his daughter with a hug, and Joel with a handshake, he declared, "Well, Captain Whitaker has made it quite clear that I have no authority here. Apparently, I am being used as a consultant only!"

Smiling indulgently, Emmie replied, "Dad, you are in the civilian world now, remember?"

"But we still value and need his expertise," Whitaker stated as he walked over to the group. Nodding his greetings to the trio waiting for him, he wasted no time launching into his lamentations about the escalating situation that was unfolding. "What in the hell is going on? Why didn't anyone recognize before now that this is probably a series of gang activities? Where do we even begin?" At the exact moment Emmie opened her mouth to reply, her phone rang. Holding up her hand to convey the message for everyone to wait, she walked a few steps away to answer the call. Whitaker continued to grumble, as André and Joel tried to calm him. Emmie ended her conversation and walked back to the men waiting for her input.

"Well," she began, "This just gets more and more interesting. My tech Sarah has been doing some research, per my request. It appears that up until about 10 years ago, the victim base seems to be random. The murders were all almost exactly in the manner they were committed, but there seemed to be no pattern with the choice of victims. Then a decade or so ago, the pattern of preying on only young, petite, dark-haired female victims emerged. Once that trend started, he, or they, have never deviated from it." Seeing the looks on the faces in the room, she nodded grimly, "Yes, I know what you are thinking…that's what I look like too!" Turning to the Captain, she calmly and soberly stated, "These killings never had anything to do with the victims. The killings were just an act of misguided sense of revenge based on targeting women who had the misfortune to reminding them of André Blanchet's daughter!"

Whitaker moved the meeting into his conference room and arranged for ice water and coffee to be served. While everyone was in the process of settling down, an officer came to the door, ushering Raj into the room. Seeing Emmie's surprised look, André explained: "I hope you don't mind me contacting someone from your team. But Raj and I worked closely on the Wright case, and I thought he may be able to add some valuable insights. Plus he is my oldest friend and right now that's important!!" Emmie shook her head and told him that she was grateful that he thought to invite Raj, and apologized for not thinking about it herself.

Joel cleared his throat; "I want to be here for this, and to do what I can. I am not sure how much I can contribute though, I am not in the same league as the rest of you!"

Emmie sharply retorted, "Yes we need you here! You are an officer of the law just like we are, in a supervisory position even, and besides, some of the crimes were committed on your turf. You are an essential part of this team."

"And an essential part of ME as well," she mused silently.

As the group reviewed the findings, André leaned toward Emmie and in sotto voce asked, "How do we profile a cult? Have you thought of that?"

Emmie shrugged and replied, "Well I guess we need to focus on the leader." Looking up at the rest of the group, she continued, "In order to profile this group of killers, we need to profile the leader. He is obviously the force behind these crimes, and if we get him, I think the others will disband."

"Do you believe that the leader is a sexual sadist?" Whitaker asked.

Nodding enthusiastically, Emmie replied, "Oh definitely! No doubt! For any of you who may not have heard of that term before, sexual sadism refers to causing pain, humiliation, fear, or some form of physical or mental harm to another person to achieve sexual gratification. I feel that this is obvious due to the sexual attacks and mutilation he or they inflicted on the victims."

"But wait!" Exclaimed Joel, "Are we talking about a person or a group of people? How can we label the whole group from the characteristics of one?"

André turned to him and replied, "You are right my friend. That is why we are profiling just the leader. He is the one that is gaining the gratification. The clan or cult he is inspiring to engage his perversions to have their own individual reasons for doing this."

Raj added, "Such as a pathological need for a sense of affiliation, a need to belong to something. This leader is probably charismatic as hell and makes his followers like somebody important and needed. This may be something these people may have been longing for their entire lives. So the leader gives them what they need, and they give him what he wants."

André chuckled and turned to his daughter, "Now you see why I thought to have him join us!"

For the benefit of Captain Whitaker and Joel, who were not familiar with profiling, Emmie launched into a brief summary of what they were looking for. "There are three major types of serial killers," she began. "They are usually characterized as Organized, Disorganized, and Mixed. An Organized killer is usually highly intelligent and well organized to the point of being meticulous. Every detail of the crime is planned out well in advance, and the killer takes every precaution to make sure they leave no incriminating evidence behind. With a Disorganized killer, most often the people they kill are in the wrong place at the wrong time. This type of serial killer appears to strike at random whenever an opportunity arises. They take no steps to cover up any signs of their crime and tend to move regularly to avoid being captured. Now, the third category of serial killers is referred to as mixed serial killers. These are the killers who cannot be easily differentiated as either organized or disorganized. With this type, there may be unexpected happenings that the criminal had not scheduled for, so the criminal may be in a position to have to change the plans or victim may fight back which may thwart the killer's plans."

Whitaker and Joel nodded their understanding, and André interjected, "But one thing we have to remember, is that a killer does not always follow the same typecasting. He may start out as an organized killer, and devolve into disorganized behaviors due to an acceleration of internal or external triggers. When an unsub, which means unknown subject, starts that downward spiral, it makes it much harder for the profilers to predict their next move."

Joel spoke up, "I understand the logic behind this, and I understand that Junior, or whoever the leader may be, is motivated by hate and revenge. I get that. But I am willing to bet that everyone in this room has been done wrong by someone, and have been pissed enough that some ugly thoughts have entered their minds. But we don't act on those thoughts! I guess what I am asking is, what makes someone a killer?"

"There are many theories," Emmie replied. "Some are those that have suffered childhood traumas, either real or just perceived. Many have serious mental illnesses, or have sociopathic tendencies, meaning they have no empathy or sense of right or wrong. Some research scientists believe that some people are genetically predisposed to be killers. Sometimes we just do not know what the trigger is! We just know there are some common characteristics."

"Exactly," stated André.

When Joel and Captain looked at him quizzically, he explained, "Well, according to history, ninety percent are male. They tend to be intelligent, but they often do poorly at school or work due to mental issues. They often come from unstable families. They are often abandoned by their fathers and raised by domineering mothers. They often hate their parents. They are often abused as a child by a family member. They have high suicide rates. From an early age, they are often interested in voyeurism, fetishism, and sado-masochistic porn. More than sixty percent have bedwetting issues past the age of twelve. They often have pyromaniacal urges. They also have a history of killing and torturing small animals at a young age." The room stayed in silence for a long moment while they processed the information given to them.

Finally, Joel spoke up, "Well, I think we don't have a moment to spare to get this bastard!"

Chapter 19

In spite of adamant protests from Emmie, the group finally managed to convince her to let Joel take her back to her house where she would have police protection. As they drove back, Emmie called her staff to obtain an update on their progress. After being informed that there was no new information, Emmie ended the disappointing call and turned to Joel. "I have all the faith in the world in my team, but damn, I am getting super frustrated. We need a break here. Soon!"

Joel glanced over at her and gently took her hand into his, and stroked it gently. "We have the best minds in the field working on this right now. We just have to be patient and be determined to nail these slime balls. Together we will do, I know that!" He exclaimed. She marveled how in the midst of all this chaos, she felt a sense of peace and happiness wash over her, just from the touch of his hand.

Arriving at Emmie's house, Joel pulled his truck up to her front door, turned off the engine, and in a series of rapid-fire movements jumped out of the vehicle and ran over to her side before she could even respond. Opening her door with a flourish, he bowed deeply and made a grand gesture with his hand, and with a mock British accent asked,

"M'lady, it would be my honor to escort you to your castle. May I have your hand so I may do so?"

Giggling like a schoolgirl, Emmie allowed him to lead her away from the truck and to her door. When they reached the entrance, Emmie joined in the fun by engaging in a deep curtsey and said, "Many thanks, kind sir." She then glanced over to the parked police car, where the officer was sitting and grinning widely. "How professional of us!! What must he be thinking?" she thought with an inner smile.

When they entered the house, Joel closed the door behind them and gently pushed her against the door and kissed her deeply. As before, Emmie felt faint from desire and want. She let the kiss linger another few seconds, then pushed him gently away. "I want you as much right now as you want me, but I think we need to hold off a bit and pour our energies into this case."

Joel nodded reluctantly, "Yeah my brain knows you are right, but my body is saying something else! But we have all the time in the world for us…like you said right now we need to focus on getting these animals!"

The next few hours were spent with Joel at his laptop and Emmie at her computer, both searching for any pertinent data while engaging in intermittent phone and video meetings with colleagues. It was starting to be that time of day in which daytime began to drift into darkness, and Emmie realized she was feeling pangs of hunger. Looking up from her work, she saw Joel intent on his screen. As though he sensed her looking at him, he raised his eyes and smiled deeply at her. "I am starved. Are you hungry at all?" she asked. When he nodded his agreement, Emmie suggested that she warm up some chicken pasta she had in the freezer. While the food was heating, Joel and Emmie sat at the kitchen counter and discussed their findings.

Joel began, "Well, I did some archive searches and chatted with a couple of old-timers who had been with the forest service for a while. The one thing that I walked away with, during this searching and talking, was that more than twenty five years ago way before my time, there were several bodies discovered in the Shenandoah Park, the same MO as the recent victim. The crime was never solved."

Startled, Emmie looked at him and asked, "All small dark-haired women?"

Nodding, he replied, "All but one. There was a male victim as well. What did you find?"

"Well," she began, "The patterns that seem to have been present with these killings indicate that the killer, or leader rather, is of the mixed organized/disorganized type. I believe that he presents with organized behaviors in the beginning, having a particular type of victim in mind, having a clear motive and plan, etc. But his passions and desire for revenge will take over dominance and will create disorganization in his actions." Joel nodded in understanding.

As Emmie stood up to get their food, Joel grabbed her by the waist and spun her around to look at him. "Ok, I am throwing caution to the wind. I am going to say it…I love you. I have totally fallen in love with you. And I want you to know that I will work with you tirelessly to find this monster. I think we make a formidable team, and this asshole doesn't have a clue what he is up against!"

Melting against him, Emmie gave him a soft kiss before replying, "I love you too. I know together we will beat him!"

After finishing their meal, Emmie suggested that they bring a plate of food and a cup of coffee out to the officer parked outside. Joel volunteered to take it out to him while she went back to her desk. A moment later he burst back through the door, his firearm drawn. Emmie jumped out of her chair and exclaimed, "What's wrong?"

"Just stay right where you are. Don't move. Please!" Joel barked, as he darted from room to room, opening closet doors, looking into cabinets and under beds. Coming back into the study where Emmie was standing looking puzzled, he took a big breath and explained, "I went out to give the officer the food. I noticed he was slumped over the wheel and not moving. I opened his car door and saw blood everywhere. It looks like his throat was cut from ear to ear. His eyes seem to have been removed and were laying on the dash. Then I found this laying on the steering wheel." He then handed her a handwritten note, along with the tissue he used to preserve evidence.

She felt her faceblanch as she read the crude handwriting, "You are as blind as this cop if you think you are safe, you bitch." They stared at each other in alarm for a moment, then Emmie broke the silence by proclaiming, "Ok this prick has pissed me off even more now. We need to get a step ahead of him, or them. If you would call Whitaker and get some uniforms out here, I will call my dad and get him up to date. They are screwing with the wrong people!"

Chapter 20

After the uniformed police, the detectives, and crime scene investigators finally cleared away, it was deep into the night. André lingered behind, along with Captain Whitaker and Raj. The senior Doctor Blanchet was understandably concerned for his daughter's safety and was articulating this to the point that Emmie was starting to consider it as Ad Nauseum. Joel stayed closely by her side but seemed to have mastered the art of showing support without being smothering, for which she was very grateful. The Captain was engaging in his usual blustery rants of frustration, which the group appeared to seem to simply overlook at this point. Raj had been silent this whole time but now cleared his throat to gain everyone's attention.

"I have a theory I want to share," he announced. "I have to warn you it may seem a little radical, but just hear me out if you will." Everyone in the room nodded in agreement. Taking a deep breath, Raj began, "Ok, we have discovered that the killings started at least thirty years ago, so that's why we came up with the multiple perpetrator theory. Brian Wright was only a small child at the time they were occurring. So we know they started with his father and continued after his arrest. We also know that although the victims now are all small young dark-haired women, that wasn't always the case. In the beginning, it was a mixed assortment of victims, but there was a majority count of petite brunettes. So, what if the target was always the females, and the others were collateral damage?"

André looked puzzled and remarked, "Ok, that's fine. That is a plausible theory. But he, or they, have made it obvious that my daughter is the main target here. The problem is, she was not even alive thirty years ago! I get where you are going with this, but there are too many holes."

Raj shook his head impatiently, "You didn't let me finish my friend. Yes, I realize that Emmie is the target now, and the other victims are merely surrogates. Yes, I understand that she was not even born thirty years ago. But what I am getting at is, someone was very angry at you, my friend. Everyone knows that the Wright woman was a good shoot, except maybe someone in that family. We know that Wright's son was part of a vendetta, he even abducted and tried to kill Emmie. We know that this was to hurt you, not her. But my friend, what if the original obsession with small, dark-haired young women started with someone else close to you and met that description? Like your wife Chloe when she was young? Maybe when she grew older and Emmie grew into adulthood, that's when the attention shifted away from Mother and onto Daughter." Emmie gasped in shock and turned to look at her father. He appeared stunned, and for once in his life was speechless.

Joel eventually broke the silence by asking, "I thought there wasn't any family left. I mean, Brian Wright had to go into foster homes because there was no one left to care for him. So who could it be?"

André regained his composure to reply, "That's what we need to figure out, and soon as possible. But you two need to head to the Bunker. I, in the meantime, am going to pay Mr. Wright a visit at USP Lee Prison!"

Chapter 21

The "Bunker" that André was referring to is a secure room set up at Quantico. It was designed similarly to a studio apartment, set up to accommodate one or two people who may need high security living arrangements for a short period of time. Emmie reluctantly agreed to stay there, and since Joel may be in danger as well due to his association with her, he was also approved to stay. They gathered some personal items and any work items they may need and were driven to the location via a SWAT team escort. Raj was to accompany them to Quantico while Emmie notified her staff and asked them to wait for her arrival. After arriving at the building, Emmie checked Joel in as a visitor and got him a badge, then they took their belongings to the Bunker. The room was simplistic but comfortable, with a bed, sofa, TV, and a kitchen area fully stocked with the basics. Joel quickly surveyed the room and asked, "Is that a security camera in here?"

Emmie chuckled softly and replied, "Yes, for safety reasons. It covers everything but the bathroom, and is visual only, no sound." She then looked at him impishly and continued, "I guess that is rather…unfortunate, isn't it?"

Joel snickered and mumbled, "Where there is a will there is a way!"

After dropping off their belongings at the Bunker, Emmie and Joel made their way to her office area. Her team was waiting as she and Joel walked into the room. Raj looked up and said, "I hope you don't mind Emmie, but I updated everyone on what was going on." Nodding in appreciation, Emmie busied herself with assigning jobs to everyone before sitting down in front of the computer herself. Even Joel was soon busy searching archives of victims found on national forest land over the last thirty years. Once everyone was immersed in their tasks, Emmie began the laborious undertaking of trying to track the Wright family tree. Deeply engrossed in her investigation, she hardly felt Sarah pull up a chair beside her. After some brief discussion on each of their individual searches, Sarah leaned closer and in a conspiratorial voice asked, "So what's the story with the hot Forest Ranger?"

Emmie felt her cheeks grow warm as she replied, "He is helping with the case since several of the bodies were found on parkland."

"Oh, is that all?" Sarah teasingly asked. "So, I guess you wouldn't mind if I made a move on him then!" As much as Emmie struggles to maintain her composure, the look on her face gave her away.

Sarah laughed and said, "I am teasing. I see the way he looks at you. All I am saying about the subject is that it's about damn time! And I am very happy for you. End of discussion." Emmie smiled gratefully at her and turned back to her searching.

Suddenly, Raj yelled from across the room, "Emmie, you need to see this!" Getting up stiffly from the seat she had been in for hours, she walked to see what he was talking about. Leaning over his shoulder she read the information he was referring to. "Dependent child Brian, age 6, will be placed in DSS custody and will be assigned a foster home, after attempts to contact deceased Mother Elizabeth Wright's twin sister Mary Peterson were unsuccessful."

Emmie gasped, "Twin sister? Why didn't anyone know about this?"

It appeared that the information Raj had uncovered was part of a Social Services archived report concerning child protective services. Further investigation showed that the reason that investigators had not realized that Elizabeth Wright had a twin sister was because they had been separated at birth. The two girls had been born out of wedlock to a heroin-addicted prostitute and had been given up for adoption at birth. They went to separate homes and never had contact with one another. Emmie grabbed the phone, and as Raj looked quizzically at her, she explained, "I am calling a judge friend of mine. I need those adoption records released now!!"

An hour later, a courier arrived at her office with a court order for the adoption agency to release all records to the FBI. Looking at his watch, Raj exclaimed, "If I leave now, I can get there before they close."

Emmie nodded her agreement as he gathered his belongings and hurried out the door. "I can see why he is Dad's best friend. I don't know what I would do without him either!" she thought.

Emmie tried calling her father to fill in him on the latest findings, but her call went straight to voice mail. "I guess he is still at the prison," she assumed. An intern was milling around, taking orders for take-out food from the local deli, and Emmie realized that they all had been so intent on their work, she had forgotten about food. She watched as Joel gave the intern his order, and found herself thinking, "Is this feeling real? Am I dreaming?" As though he was reading her thoughts, he looked up and gave her a meaningful look from across the room. Emmie felt a warm rush flood over her and she smiled at him. When she broke eye contact, she looked around and saw Sarah looking at her grinning widely. She tried to shoot her a warning glare but realized that the smile on her face was incongruent with any sort of reprimand. At that moment the phone rang with a call from her father. Answering the call, she spoke to him for several minutes and when she ended the call, she asked her staff and Joel to gather around for a quick briefing. "As you know, my father was going to the Federal Prison to see if he could meet with Wright Senior," she began. "He was able to see him and he said that apparently, thirty years in prison mellowed him out. He was truly cooperative and seemed forthcoming with information. He told my dad that he and his wife had found out about her twin only about six months before his capture and arrest. Wright went on to say that his wife and her sister connected quite a few times before his arrest and her death." After taking a brief pause, Emmie continued, "Now get this…Wright strongly implied that his wife not only knew about his activities but also participated in some of them. He also revealed that once his wife and her sister met, they immediately formed a very close bond."

Kaitlyn, who once was a homicide detective, stated, "Well the plot sure seems to be thickening, doesn't it? This makes it more important that we find this woman."

Emmie nodded in agreement, "Yes it does. We may know more as soon as we hear back from Raj."

As the group gathered to have their meal, they continued with the discussion of possible theories and ideas. Raj called in just as they were finishing their dinner. Emmie put him on speaker so the group could hear him. "Well, I did manage to make it to the adoption agency before they closed. The front desk staff hemmed and hawed a bit, but after I flashed the signed court order at them, they gave me copies of the documents I asked for. It appears that the twins were sent separately to families who adopted them. Elizabeth was adopted by the Devereaux family, and Mary became a part of the Peterson household. I have the address for the Petersons, and I will make a trip first thing in the morning to see them. I don't think they would appreciate me showing up at their home at 11 at night!" he chuckled.

Emmie filled him in on the information her father had gained from his visit to the prison, then bade him Good Night. She then turned to her staff and announced, "I didn't realize it was this late, you guys are the best for working tirelessly and never complaining. Go home, get some sleep, we will meet back here in the morning."

Emmie and Joel headed to the Bunker to get some rest. Joel scowled at the security camera, much to Emmie's amusement. "You know, we need to rest so we will be alert for the case tomorrow anyhow," she laughed.

"I know," he petulantly replied, "But I just hate the idea of someone sitting there watching our every move." She assured him that in most cases there was not a designated person watching the camera in the room, that it was primarily to be played back in the event that something happened, and that the camera outside the Bunker was the only one under surveillance. Somewhat reassured, Joel eased his tall frame onto the sofa and turned the TV on low. Emmie went to go take a warm shower to relax before bed. As the warm currents ran soothingly over her sore tense muscles, she felt the grime of the day wash from her body. When she felt her humanity return, she dried off and put on the government-issued robe that was provided. Joel announced that he needed the shower as well, and disappeared into the bathroom. Emmie stretched out on the bed and began to feel very sleepy when she was brought back to alertness by Joel's warm, moist body climbing next to her and nuzzling her neck. Startled, she protested, "Joel, the camera!" Grinning widely, he silently pointed at the surveillance device, now completely shrouded in his shirt. Laughing with delight, she noted that sleep was overrated anyhow, and fell into his embrace.

In spite of their adventurous evening, the amorous couple was up early the next morning to resume their pursuit. Robert and Sarah were just walking in, Raj was headed to the adoptive family's home, and Shawn and Kaitlyn were already hard at work in the field. Coffee had been brewed, and there was a platter of breakfast sandwiches and fruit in the break room. The morning sped by without much ado, and André stopped in for a while to review his prison visit. When he got up to leave, Emmie walked her father to the elevator. Before pressing the button, he turned to her and exclaimed, "I know this whole ordeal has been rough on you, but I have to tell you, your mother and I are so proud of the person you have become. We both think you are fabulous!" Emmie's eyes misted over as she gave her father a warm hug and they said their goodbyes. As she walked back to her office, she received a text from Raj. "Met with the family, they know where Mary is. Quite interesting story. They went to the other room to get me the address now. Call you in a minute when I leave." Encouraged, she went back into the room with the others and told them there was a significant breakthrough, and Raj would be calling with details in a minute or two. There was finally some promising news!!

After about an hour, and Emmie still hadn't heard back from Raj, she began to grow impatient. When she placed a call to him, it went straight to his voice mail. A nagging uneasy feeling began to gnaw at her. Walking over to Sarah, she asked if Raj's phone could be traced. Sarah put in his data, then shook her head. "I can't, his phone is off. When you turn off your phone, it will stop communicating with nearby cell towers and can be traced only to the location it was in when it was powered down. It appears that it was powered down about 45 minutes ago, and the last known address was in Dumfries Virginia," she reported.

"What is at that address?" Emmie inquired.

Sarah punched a few more keystrokes, paused, and then turned to Emmie. Wide-eyed she exclaimed, "It is the town landfill site!"

Both FBI and local police rushed to the landfill to search for any clues. Emmie notified her father concerning this latest development and he assured her he would be at Quantico in a few minutes.. Emmie picked up her phone to call Captain Whitaker to ask if he had further information, but before she could place the call, a call actually came through from him.

"Dr. Blanchet? This is Captain Whitaker. We have found Agent Patel's phone, it appeared to have been discarded at the landfill. At this time we have not found him or have any leads as to where he could be. But please be assured we are making this a priority." Emmie thanked him and ended the call. She updated the team and Joel about the call and then busied herself with paperwork in an attempt to calm herself and gather her thoughts. When she realized that was futile, she left the area and headed back to the Bunker for a moment. Joel was occupied and did not notice her leaving, which was Emmie secretly glad of. She loved him but she just needed to regroup alone. Entering the room, she sat at the edge of the bed, closed her eyes, and practiced her relaxation techniques. As she focused on her breathing, she allowed her mind to wander to what she always used as her "safe place"; the mountain lake where her family had a cabin. As she imagined the mirror finish of the pristine water, the sound of the rustling leaves on the trees, the comforting feel of sunlight on her skin, and the smell of the fresh crisp air. Emmie felt herself melting into a healing state of relaxation. But this time when she exercised her mental imagery, Joel was there with her, holding her hand, walking through the woods, playing in the water. A sense of profound peace washed over her, and for a brief moment, the outside world with its challenges and chaos seemed to cease to exist. Abruptly, Emmie was brought back to reality by the shrill sound of sirens as emergency vehicles rushed by on the streets below, hurrying to some unknown crisis somewhere. Chuckling, she stretched and thought, "Ok, the real world beckons. But that was nice while it lasted."

As Emmie re-entered the work area, Joel looked up at her curiously. She smiled at him reassuringly and scanned the room. Everyone was engrossed in what they were doing and hardly noticed that she had briefly left. As she was sliding into her seat, Shawn came to her desk. For someone very muscular from his years as serving as a Navy Seal, he nevertheless moved deftly and almost stealthily, and Emmie almost never heard him approaching. "Did you hear about the bombing?" he inquired. When she shook her head in denial, he continued, "Yea, it was a car bombing about four blocks from here. No witnesses or suspects. No one is claiming responsibility for it, so we don't think it was a terrorist act. Right now it is being viewed as a single attack."

Before Emmie could reply, the elevator door opened and her father emerged. He appeared rumpled and distraught. She rushed to him and asked what was wrong. André looked at her and muttered, "C'était ma voiture! La bombe! Ils ont essayé de me tuer!" (That was my car! The bomb! They tried to kill me!)

Emmie gasped and threw her arms around him, "Oh my God! Are you OK? How? How are you OK?"

André was visibly shaken when he replied, "I was leaving the coffee shop to come here. I walked to the car and realized that I had left my pastry on the counter. You know how scatterbrained I can be about those things! Anyhow, I went back to get it and decided to press the unlock from the key fob as I was headed back into the shop. All I heard was a huge boom and felt myself being propelled forward into the side of the building. I always joke about

91

my absentminded behavior, but this time it saved my life."

Emmie didn't realize that Joel was now standing next to her until he placed his hand on her shoulder reassuringly. Glancing up at him she saw the concern in his face. They both led André to a seat, and Joel went to get him some water. While they waited for investigators to come to interview him, Emmie updated him about what was going on with Raj. André shook his head with concern, "My daughter was abducted and almost killed, my best friend is missing, and someone just tried to blow me to smithereens. The fallout from this case is never going to end. I am so glad that your mother left last week to visit her parents in France. I miss her but at least I know she is safe."

Chapter 22

Several hours had passed and there still was no word about Raj. The first 24-hours in a missing person situation are the most crucial, and Emmie and the team were feeling the pressure. All parties involved were giving this case their full attention, and everyone was working tirelessly trying to come up with some viable facts. As Emmie sat sipping a cup of chai, her favorite hot beverage, the elevator sounded again and Whitaker and one of his lead detectives walked in. The Captain had a grim expression on his face as he strode purposefully across the room to Emmie. "Do you by any chance know what Agent Patel was wearing when he left this office yesterday?" He asked. Emmie shook her head and looked inquiringly at the team.

Kaitlyn spoke up, "I do. I was teasing him because he was wearing that awful plaid shirt that we always say looks like a tablecloth." Whitaker looked even more stern than usual when he showed Kaitlyn a photo on his phone and asked if this was the shirt. She gasped and nodded wordlessly. Turning to Emmie, the captain explained that the shirt was found at the landfill, soaked in blood. He had sent it to the lab to have the blood tested and to be examined for any other DNA. Emmie fought back tears as countless scenarios flew through her head. This killer, or killers, seemed to be able to anticipate their every move and acted accordingly. That is: her leaving the ME's office when she was abducted, Raj disappearing when he went to follow a lead, and her father almost being blown up when he was coming to share information with her. It seemed like the perpetrators were inside their heads!

Shaking off her negative feelings, Emmie buried herself in your work. Her father was still in the building, and his concern was obvious despite his stoic mannerisms. "Do you have any idea at all what he discovered when he went to the Peterson home?" he inquired of his daughter.

"No," she replied. "He just texted me that he had information and knew where Mary was, and that he was going to send me the info when he left the Peterson residence. That's the last I heard from him," as she choked back tears. Sitting next to her, Joel discreetly took her hand and squeezed it under the table. She clutched it briefly, signifying that she appreciated the gesture of support. "I feel that we need to try to retrace his steps and see if we can find that address, and make a trip to the residence ourselves," she offered.

"No WE about it, dear daughter. You are sequestered here. You can send someone from your team or even a detective from the local police." When Emmie glared at him and started to protest, "I know I have no authority here, but I am your father. I am not letting you take a crazy risk like this. If you insist on arguing with me, I will talk to my friend, the Director, and ask him to send you to a safe house someplace where you won't be able to work at all!" he continued firmly.

Nodding reluctantly, she turned away, muttering under her breath, "Bossy old man."

"I heard that!" he chuckled as he walked out of the room.

As the day progressed, the tension in the room was growing thick enough to be almost visible. There was almost a sense of desperation in the environment, to find the killer, to find Raj before it was too late, to just find a lead to follow. As Emmie continued to scour the web, she suddenly had a thought. Turning in her chair, she called for Sarah. As her savvy tech came over to her, she asked, "I don't know why I didn't think of this before, but is there any way you can search Raj's phone and see what his location was when he sent that last text to us?"

Sarah's eyes widened as she exclaimed, "Oh Lord! That never even occurred to me! Duh!" Her finger flew over the keyboard as she worked her magic. "Yes!" she exclaimed. "I have the address he texted you from!"

Emmie gave her a quick hug of gratitude, then made the arrangements for Kaitlyn and Shawn to head to that address. She also called Whitaker who said he would head there himself with some of the detectives helping with the case. Feeling invigorated by now to have a direction to follow, Emmie threw herself headlong into her work. Only about 30 minutes had passed when her phone rang and she picked up a call from Whitaker. "Are you sure that was the address your tech said the text message was from?" He asked gruffly. "Well of course I am. Sarah is the best," he replied in a slightly irritable tone.

"Well we have a problem then," the captain continued, "There is not a residence at that address, in fact, it's a neighborhood park. Plus no one in the neighborhood has even heard of the Petersons!"

Emmie's mind was reeling with thoughts after she hung up. Why would Raj have said he was texting her from the residence when in reality he was at a park? She decided to call the adoption agency and get the information herself that Raj had retrieved. Since there was a court order to disclose information, the agency should be compelled to provide this to her. However, she was dumbfounded when the receptionist informed her that they had never been issued an order, nor had they even spoken to or seen anyone from the FBI. Emmie asked to speak to a supervisor, who confirmed that no one had approached them, but assured her that they would gladly release the information as soon as they saw some paperwork. Puzzled and concerned, Emmie went through the embarrassing process of asking the judge to have the order reissued, and arranged for Shawn to pick it up and go to the adoption agency.

Seeing her father talking to Joel, Emmie walked over and asked them to follow her into a private room. Closing the door behind them, she turned to the two men in her life and exclaimed, "I have no clue what the hell is going on! My freaking head is spinning!" She then proceeded to explain in detail her latest discoveries concerning Raj, and her confusion and apprehensions. When she finished, André looked at her silently for a second, and when he spoke, it was in a tone she had never heard before.

"Are you actually suggesting that Raj may be implicated in some way? Do you understand what you are saying? He has been my best friend before you were even born. He was there at your christening. He served with me at Interpol. We had each other's backs more times than I could ever count. Now you are suggesting that he isn't the person we know that he is? I refuse to believe this, and although I know you are desperate to solve this case, I highly suggest you look deeper before you sully the name of one of the best men that I have had the honor of knowing!" Standing up abruptly, Andrés stalked out the door. Emmie sat in stunned silence.

Joel placed his hand gently on her shoulder, "Please try not to take this to heart. He is just overwhelmed by what you have told him. He needs to absorb and process this." Emmie nodded silently, fighting back tears. "When is this ever going to end," she thought.

Emmie spent the next several hours pondering every possible alternate theory to their findings. Although she was crushed by her father's reaction to her, she fully understood it. She did not want to imagine that the man who has been like an uncle to her for her entire life could be someone she didn't know after all. But no matter how much she deliberated, she was having difficulty coming up with a more favorable theory. As she was deep in thought, her email notification emitted an alert, and she opened it to find that she had a report from the lab. With a sinking feeling, she read that the blood found on Raj's shirt did not match his DNA on file. "What is happening here?" she reflected. Just then, her father purposefully strode into the room and announced, "Ma chere, I am sorry for my behavior earlier. But you need to understand this man is like a brother to me. I see where the evidence is heading, but there has to be another answer out there."

Emmie leaped out of her chair and embraced her parent with a quick hug. "I know. I do not want to believe this either. I have been obsessing about other possibilities. But the facts keep stacking up. I just found out that the blood on his shirt is not his. I don't know what to think anymore!" At that moment, Shawn walked into the room. He looked very somber. Taking in Emmie and André with a glance, he said, "I am sorry if I am interrupting, but I don't think this can wait. I just got back from the adoption agency, and I have the records for the twin sisters." Motioning for Shawn to take a seat, Emmie waited expectantly for him to begin. He slid the folder over to his boss, stating: "I looked at them briefly in the car, but I am sure you want to study them in detail."

Silence enveloped the room as Emmie pored over the documents for several minutes. Finally, she looked up and began, "Well, the records show that Elizabeth was adopted to the Devereaux family, as we knew. Mary was placed with Ronald and Janet Peterson, and they did live in the town of Dumfries, but not at the address Raj texted us from. It also states that the family had a biological daughter as well, about a year older than Mary. Her name is Ronette. Shawn, can you take this info to Sarah and have her search to see if she can find out anything about the parents and the two girls?" Emmie smiled at him gratefully as he took the folder to follow her instructions.

Just a few minutes later, Emmie received a text from Sarah that she had some information. With André in tow, she walked to the main work area. Joel and the team appeared to have been waiting for her. In her efficient manner, Sarah had found that Ronald and Janet Peterson had died in a house fire several years ago. The fire was considered suspicious and had been under investigation. The results of the said investigation were inconclusive and the search was dropped. Mary Peterson appeared to have been a troubled child, and as an adult lived an uneventful life until she dropped off the grid approximately a decade ago. Ronette Peterson was alive and well, living and working as a nurse in Alexandria at Inova Mount Vernon Hospital. Emmie felt a rush of excitement at these findings, and asked, "Do we have a number and address for Ms. Ronette?"

Sarah nodded and replied, "I am sending it to your phones now."

"Ok," Emmie exclaimed, "Let's go talk to her."

André started to protest, but before he could utter the words, his daughter looked at him and declared, "I cannot take another minute of this house arrest shit. I am going to talk to her. If you guys are that worried, then come with me! Either way, I am going."

Shawn looked at her intently, and stated quietly, "Damn right I am coming with you. I will get the Suburban brought around now."

When the crew gathered into the agency vehicle, it was Shawn, Joel, and Kaitlyn that accompanied Emmie on her quest. Sarah and Robert stayed behind to process any additional data, and André went back to his office to tend to some business. Since Ms. Peterson lived only a few blocks from the hospital she was employed at, Emmie decided that it would be most efficient for her and Joel to be dropped off at the hospital while Shawn and Kaitlyn checked out the residence and neighborhood. It was starting to rain lightly when Shawn let them out at the hospital entrance. Sarah had discovered that Ronette was a cardiology nurse who worked in the post-surgery unit. They followed the signs leading them to the correct area and took the elevator to the fourth floor. Directly across from the elevator was the nurses' station, at which they stopped and inquired as to whether Ronette was working today. They were assured that she was, but was with a patient and would be available soon. Only a few minutes elapsed before a blonde, slightly chubby but attractive nurse in her fifties emerged from one of the rooms. As she approached the station, one of the nurses said something to her and pointed to Emmie and Joel. The nurse looked as though she wanted to bolt, but then appeared to think better of it and slowly and tentatively walked over to them. Emmie took a couple steps toward her, and held out her credentials, "Ronette Peterson? I am Dr. Emmanuelle Blanchet with the FBI, and this is my associate Joel McNeil with the National Forest Service. We need to ask you a few questions. Is there someplace private we can talk?"

Nodding in agreement, Ronette held up a hand to wait, then walked over to the nurses' station and spoke for a moment with her co-workers, then came back to where they were waiting. She signaled for them to follow her, and she led to a small vacant patient room, where they entered. Ronette closed the door behind them, gestured for them to sit, then took a seat herself on one of the beds. She sat quietly and looked at them expectantly. Emmie spoke first, "I am sure you are curious as to why we are here today, Ms. Peterson."

Ronette shook her head slowly, "No. Not really. I have been expecting you for years. I just didn't know when."

Surprised by that remark, Emmie looked at her quizzically and asked her what she meant. Ronette raised her eyes to meet hers, and replied, "Well I am assuming you are here because of Mary, right? I will tell you anything I know, but I haven't seen her in years, since she killed my parents."

Chapter 23

Taken aback by the woman's candor, Emmie and Joel stared wordlessly for a second at her. It was Emmie who broke the silence, "Please tell us what you mean by that." In a quiet voice, Ronette continued, "Mary was always a problem child. My parents worked very hard to make sure that both of us were treated as equals, even though she was adopted. When she was old enough to understand, probably around age five, they explained to her that although she did not come out of Mommy's belly, she was CHOSEN to be with them, so was very special and loved. But it didn't seem to matter how hard my parents worked at trying to make her feel like she belonged, she continually rebelled. She was sent to the best counselors available but continued to carry this huge chip on her shoulder. It got even worse when she was in her teens, she actually would become abusive to them and me. By the time of the fire that took Mom and Dad's lives, we both had left the home. I was in college and she was...God knows where...here and there. Living on different friend's sofas. The morning of the fire, Mary came to see our parents, wanting another handout. I know this because when I called home later, Mom was in tears over the way Mary had talked to her. I reassured her that she did the right thing by turning her down. Later that night, I got the call about the fire. I never talked to her again."

Joel was the first to speak after Ronette finished. "That sounds like she should have been the main suspect. Why wasn't she?"

Ronette shook her head impatiently, "Oh she was! They wanted so badly to get her for it. But it ended up that she had what they called an airtight alibi. She was at a party in which several people attested that she was there the whole time. So she got away with murdering my precious parents," and wiped away a tear.

Emmie patted her hand to comfort her and thanked her for her meeting with them. "One more question, I know you haven't talked to her since that incident, but have you heard anything from others about her?"

Ronette shook her head, then paused before replying, "Well sort of. I heard years ago that that somehow she managed to find out that she had a birth twin, and found her. According to the grapevine, she was obsessed with this sister when she found her and was seriously starting to turn her life around for the better. Then the sister got killed by the police. Came to find out the sister was married to that horrible serial killer who murdered all those girls. I heard she went totally crazy when her sister died, and disappeared completely."

After thanking her again for her cooperation, Emmie and Joel left the hospital. Shawn and Kaitlyn were waiting for them when they walked out the door. Kaitlyn spoke up as they entered the vehicle. "Well, that was a colossal waste of time. We found nothing." Emmie assured them their visit had been informative and filled her co-workers in on their meeting.

Joel spoke up when she had finished, "But, if Mary had 'gone crazy' like Ronette said, there should be a record of her being in mental hospitals, right?"

"Absolutely," Emmie replied, "I will get Sarah on that now," as she picked up her phone.

On the ride back to Quantico, Emmie updated Robert and Sarah on the latest developments and asked Sarah to do a search at all mental health facilities for the last thirty years. She then called her father and brought him up to speed. After completing those tasks, she dealt with her troubling thoughts involving the fact that there was still no word of Raj, and everyone's concern was peaking. Was he somehow involved in this? Or was he just an unfortunate victim? Both scenarios were overwhelmingly negative! She felt like her brain was in overdrive and didn't know how to shut it down. As though Joel was reading her thoughts, he reached over and held her hand gently. She turned to look at him and saw him gazing intently at her. Throughout time it has been said that the eyes are the window to the soul, and when Emmie peered into Joel's eyes, she imagined she could see into the very depths of his being. Silently, she marveled at how he seemed to have the ability to reach her inner self and create calmness, even in the middle of chaos. Suddenly, she realized that the vehicle was no longer moving, was startled to discover they were back at Quantico, and her colleagues were looking at them and grinning from ear to ear. Mumbling something about everyone needing to get to work, she scurried out of the vehicle and up to her office.

Sarah saw her as she entered the office area, and her face lit up with excitement. "I couldn't find any records of Mary Peterson. Then I decided to search public records for name changes and Bingo!! Shortly after the death of her sister Elizabeth from the police gunfire, Mary changed her name to Beth Blanchard, who does show as being admitted several times over the last few decades to facilities for the mentally ill."

Emmie looked at her with surprise and exclaimed, "Wow…ok, so the name Beth is to try to emulate her now deceased twin, but Blanchard? Do you think she…?"

Before she could complete her sentence, André, who had walked up behind her without her realizing it, finished the statement. "Yes my dear, she was taking on a bastardized form of our last name!"

"What the hell?" Joel interjected. "Was she trying to be a hybrid of her sister and your family?"

Shaking her head, Emmie announced, "I need Whitaker here and gather the team. We need to discuss a profile."

When everyone was present, Emmie stood up before the group and launched into her speech. "I know we have discussed a profile previously, but a lot of additional data has been discovered. We know that Brian Wright was not acting alone. We now know that Elizabeth Wright had a twin sister, separated at birth, and reunited shortly before her death by police fire. We recently found out that the twin, Mary Peterson disappeared after the death, and changed her name. Per her adoptive sister, she reacted strongly to her twin's death, even though they had only recently met. She changed her name to Beth Blanchard, which indicates she assumed a derivative of her deceased sister's name of

Elizabeth. Much to our dismay, it appears that she took the last name of Blanchard to imitate our family name of 'Blanchet.' We cannot find any address for her but have discovered records showing her hospitalized several times, with diagnoses of Delusional Disorder—Persecutory Type, Borderline Personality Disorder, and Anti-Social Personality Disorder. Considering her mental health issues, and her aggressive behaviors in the past, she is definitely a person of interest. We feel she may have worked in partnership with someone to commit the killings that occurred after Wright Senior's death. We need to focus all of our attention on finding the whereabouts of this woman."

Silence lay in the room like a blanket of leaden heaviness. Captain Whitaker broke the quiet when he questioned "Do you think she had anything to do with Agent Patel's disappearance?" Emmie felt her voice break when she replied, "God I hope not! We need to find him, and soon. But right now our focus must be on searching for Mary Peterson, aka Beth Blanchard. Hopefully, if we find her, we may find a clue as to where Raj is. Sarah, please arrange a press conference. The media can sometimes be a good resource. Shawn and Robert, check the hospital records and see what their discharge paperwork reveals. Kaitlyn, if you would, see if you can get her juvie records released, and see what can be derived from that." Her team nodded in agreement and set off to fulfill their tasks.

André had entered the room during Emmie's announcement, and declared, "I would like to be with you for the press release if you don't mind. In the meantime, I am going to scour over my old files and see if I missed anything."

Emmie nodded to an agreement, then turned to Joel. "Would you go over the files of the bodies that were found on national forest land, and see if they differ in any way from the bodies found elsewhere?"

"Of course," he nodded. "Anything else?"

She smiled and replied, "Just keep reassuring me that you are not a dream!"

The press release went smoothly, with Emmie giving the reporters details of Mary Peterson, along with a photo that Robert had found in some old hospital admission records. Andrés helped by filling in some of the blanks regarding the history of the original case. Emmie and Joel were taking a brief break having some tea and coffee, when Kaitlyn yelled across the room, "Em, they found her!" Rushing to Kaitlyn's desk, with Joel and André in tow, Kaitlyn continued, "There was a call a few minutes ago from a motel clerk. After seeing the photo on the news, he is certain she is a guest in one of the rooms there."

"Ok!" Emmie declared. "Let's get SWAT involved, call Whitaker, and let's go get our woman!"

When everyone arrived at the fleabag motel, the suspect was allegedly staying at, Emmie and Captain Whitaker went into the office. The desk clerk was a scrawny male in his early twenties with acne marked skin. He announced that he was the one who called, and the woman he called about had registered as Beth Blanchard, looked like the photo shown on the news, and was in room thirty-two.

"Is she there now?" Whitaker asked. The clerk nodded nervously, then stammered, "B-b-but there is something else." Impatiently, Whitaker gestured for him to continue. "The maid tried to go in to clean a few minutes ago. No one answered when she knocked, so she used her key to let herself in. The guest was sitting on her bed and had several guns on the bed next to her. The maid apologized and quickly left. She is pretty shaken up."

Whitaker stormed out and strode over to the SWAT team to inform them that the situation had escalated to a more dangerous one. Emmie grabbed his arm to get his attention, "We need to keep her alive. She is the only one who can give us the information we need about the killers. Plus, she may know what happened to Raj." Whitaker nodded reluctantly and continued to approach SWAT. Emmie turned back to walk to her team to update them on their findings.

Since they now knew that the suspect was armed, a parameter was set up about fifty feet from the motel room. Whitaker handed Emmie the megaphone, and she took it and raised it to her mouth. "Mary Peterson, or Beth Blanchard. This is the FBI. The local police and SWAT are here as well. So, that means you are surrounded. We don't want to hurt you. Please come out with your hands on your head so we can talk." Suddenly, the glass shattered as shots were fired from within the room. SWAT became poised to commence firing, waiting for the command. Emmie yelled to Whitaker, "Tell them to stand down!! We need her alive!" Again, she appealed to the woman inside to be reasonable to come out of the building, whom they just wanted to talk. In reply, there was another shot, which appeared to remain inside the room.

Whitaker shouted, "Screw this shit, we are going in," and gave the command for SWAT to storm the room. The officers pushed forward using their shields as protection, and a battering ram to break down the door. When they gained entry, they stopped and called for Emmie and Whitaker to come forward. When they entered the shabbily decorated room, they immediately saw a woman matching the description of Mary Peterson, lying dead on the floor from a self-induced gunshot wound to the forehead.

CSI was called, along with the ME. Emmie went back outside and perched dejectedly on a nearby bench. "What now? With her dead, we may never get the answers we need," she mused.

Joel came over and stood close to her, their arms touching. "I know you feel discouraged, but we will catch a break sooner or later, we have to."

Shaking off her dark mood, she smiled tightly at him and nodded, "Yea, I know. We just need to keep trying. Let's go back into the motel office and see if the clerk has anything else he may have seen." Together they walked back to see the nervous employee.

He appeared pallid and shaky. "That woman is dead because of me," he muttered. Emmie reassured him that he had done the right thing, and that woman was dead because she shot herself, end of story. She then asked him if he was sure there wasn't anything else he could remember about the woman. He shook his head in denial, then hesitated and stated, "Well she had a boyfriend, does that matter?" When they urged him to continue, he said, "Yea some Indian dude, about fifty or so. He would come to her room at night and leave early before dawn. We figured he was trying not to be seen, like maybe he was married or something." Shaken deeply, Emmie looked at Joel, then took out her phone, flipping through pictures until she found one of Raj.

"Is this him?" she asked the clerk.

He looked at the photo for a second and nodded vigorously, "Oh yea, that's him all right. He has been here every night since she checked in. I tried to be friendly whenever I saw him, but he would just lower his head and keep walking. Like I said, he didn't want to be seen!"

Emmie walked back to their vehicle with her head held low, so no one could see the tears streaming down her cheeks. Joel walked helplessly beside her, not knowing what to do to comfort her. When they reached their destination, Joel grabbed her and pulled her behind the vehicle, where the others could not see them. "Emmie, I know your mind must be whirling right now. But maybe there is some sort of explanation. We will figure this out. But until then, we do need to update everyone, even your dad. We need all the help we can get." Looking up at him through teary eyes, she nodded slightly. As Joel pulled her toward him and hugged her closely, Kaitlyn and Shawn walked up to the vehicle.

Kaitlyn saw them first and joked "Hey you love bir…," trailing off when she saw Emmie's tear-stained face. She had never seen her boss break down like this before, and she was at a loss for words.

Emmie rubbed the tears away angrily, and snapped, "I will fill everyone in when we get back to the office. Gather everyone, we are leaving now."

Chapter 24

When they arrived back at Quantico, Emmie gathered the team and briefed them on the latest findings. She had managed to compose herself on the trip back, so she was able to deliver the speech without visible emotion. When she finished, she asked Robert to inform Captain Whitaker of what had occurred. As she sat at her desk, she was overwhelmed with an enormous sense of fatigue, as though her life source has been drained from her very being. She felt a wave of nostalgia and longing for her own jetted tub and comfortable bed. With an air of determination, she got up from her seat and went over to Joel. "I want my own house. I want to be where I am comfortable. Please don't try to talk me out of it. I don't feel like I can be here another minute."

He gazed at her for a long moment and seemed to read something in her face. Nodding, he said, "Ok, finish up what you need to now. I will get our stuff and be back in a minute." Smiling gratefully, Emmie busied herself gathering some things from her desk, then heading over to the team to notify them what was going on.

Shawn spoke up, "We understand and think it is the best for you right now. We will make sure there is security at your home, and there won't be a repeat of what happened to that police officer. And we are only a call away if you need us." After quick hugs all around, Emmie turned away. Joel had just returned with their belongings, so they walked together to his truck.

When they reached it, Emmie stopped and cried, "I just don't know what to say. I have known him my whole life. I haven't even told Dad yet. I wonder if he will believe me now."

Emmie felt a sense of relief when she walked through her front door. She set the security code for the doors and windows, then walked into her bedroom to unpack. Joel entered the room and sat at the edge of the bed, gazing at her. As she turned to look at him, all the emotions of the past few days washed over her like a dam that had just burst at its seams. Wordlessly, she swiftly walked over to him and kissing him passionately, began to tear off his clothing and hers as well. Animal lust was all she knew at this moment, as she straddled him and lowered herself onto him. As she rode him on the path to ecstasy, everything negative that had happened over the last few days disappeared. Their moans built to a crescendo as they both exploded in climax together.

Later as they lie together in the warm bath, and the soothing jets of water pulsated against them, Joel stroked her hair and chuckled. Emmie looked at him puzzled. "Well, I guess we really wanted each other, huh?" he teased.

She fumbled with her words, "I more than wanted you and I needed you. I needed to feel, well, how you make me feel."

Nuzzling the nape of her neck, he replied with a sexy growl, "Woman, you make me have feelings I didn't even know existed before I met you."

Smiling up at him, she responded, "I have a good idea that there are many more feelings we still have to explore!" Joel grinned widely, "Yes we do. But right now I have a question for you. Are you as hungry as I am? I know Luigi's down the street is still open, but I would have to go run to pick it up. You OK with Italian?"

Emmie nodded in agreement, "Sounds perfect."

After they got out of the tub and dressed, Joel called in the food order while Emmie looked over some news clippings from earlier Wright-related killings. Before Joel left to pick up the food, he gave Emmie a gentle hug and kiss. She handed him a key and a slip of paper, telling him that she may fall asleep and this way he could get in and disarm the code. As she heard his truck pull away, she settled down on her sofa. Just like she anticipated, she started to feel very sleepy. Her drowsiness was interrupted by the ring of her phone. The ID showed that it was her father. "Oh Lord, I can't delay it any longer, I am going to have to tell him what is going on," she thought. She picked up the phone but before she could say hello, Andrés excitedly cut in, "Emmie, I have wonderful news. Please get here as soon as you can. I am still at the office. I need to tell you, in person!" Feeling that it was probably better to tell him what she needed to face to face anyhow, she agreed to come over. Stretching the sleepiness away, she threw on a pair of jeans and a tee, and put her silky dark hair up in a messy bun. Looking in the mirror, she thought, "Good enough for this time of day!" She left a text for Joel, telling him she needed to run out and that she would be right back to join him in dinner. He did not reply so she assumed he was probably either driving or in the restaurant.

The drive to André's office was only a few blocks away, but enough time for Emmie to be able to brush off her grogginess and focus on how to tell her father that his lifelong best friend appears to be implicated in a string of heinous crimes. How could she make him accept and understand something that she couldn't either? Since it was after business hours, the building was dark when she arrived. She pressed the front door security button, and her father promptly buzzed her in. Without the usual bright lights and flurry of activity, the building seemed unnaturally quiet, almost eerie. Reaching the floor where André's offices were, she could hear voices coming from his headquarters. As she walked into his waiting area, André rushed from his office, grabbed her hand, and declared, "Come, Come, I have a wonderful surprise!" Curious, she allowed herself to be led into his office. A man was standing with his back to her, pouring a drink from the decanter on the stand. Turning around to face her, she gasped as she looked in the face of Raj Patel.

Seeing the stunned look on his daughter's face, André gleefully exclaimed, "I knew that everyone was wrong, that there was a logical explanation for Raj's disappearance. He just had a family emergency and also misplaced his phone. Once he explained everything to me, he asked that I call you over here so he could reassure you that all is well. Now we can all breathe easier!! Isn't that right my friend?" Raj did not answer but stared coldly at Emmie, his eyes glimmering with an unidentifiable emotion. Clearing her throat, Emmie asked softly, "Do you want to tell us about Mary Peterson?" He looked at her silently, then turned and walked toward to door. When he reached it, he stood with his back to the door, and pulled a snubnosed revolver out of his pocket, pointing it at Emmie and her father.

"What the fuck?" André exclaimed.

Glaring at them with snake-like cold eyes, he ordered them both to sit. When they complied, he began to speak in a curt, low tone, biting off each word as though they were being fueled by pure hate. "What about Mary Peterson? I will tell you about her. I have been waiting thirty years to tell you about her. She was the love of my life. You may say she was mentally ill, I say she was energetic and interesting. We met at a party, and we were drawn to one another like a moth to a flame. She kept me uplifted, kept me feeling alive. I wanted to marry her, but my mother was alive at the time and would have disowned me if I had married a white girl. Plus, Mary was too free-spirited for the tradition of marriage anyhow. We had been together for about three years when she found that she had a twin sister. She became obsessed with finding her and relentlessly searched until she found her. Her twin was Elizabeth Wright, yes, THAT Elizabeth Wright. But then, you know that don't you? Anyhow, her efforts finally paid off, she located her, and they met up. They bonded immediately. It is like they fulfilled the stories about the connection that identical twins have. They were only together for a few months when Jonathan Wright was discovered to be the Darwin Killer. I had just found out and was deliberating whether to tell Mary or not. I chose not to. That night, a team raided the Wright residence, arrested him, and shot

Elizabeth. Mary was never the same. It was like I lost her that night. I don't think she ever smiled again. She became bitter and miserable, and suffered from delusions."

André interrupted, "But Raj, you know that was a necessary shot, I did what I had to do. She came after us!"

Raj's face turned livid in rage. "Shut the hell up!! I know what was determined. No one was going to blame you, not the holy André Blanchet, the superhero of the agency! Elizabeth was a necessary kill, and Mary's resulting trauma was collateral damage. Collateral damage. Because of you."

Emmie spoke up, "But Raj, we have worked together for a couple of years now, and you have been like family, why…."

Raj smiled evilly and said, "If nothing else, I am a patient man. I played the role of best friend and colleague. I came to the birthday parties and graduations. I bided my time. The whole time hating the two of you with every fiber of my being. Waiting for the time I could get even with you. In spite of Mary changing so after her twin's death, we did share one common passion, our hatred of your father. We watched his career soar, his marriage thrive, and his life being complete when you were born. While we waited for our opportunity to destroy your father, we satisfied our hunger for revenge by choosing surrogates that resembled Chloe, and then later when you grew up, those who looked like you. Sometimes others got in the way, and they had to be eliminated as well. They were, as you say, collateral damage."

"So you two have been doing all these killings?" André asked.

Raj sneered, and replied, "For many years, yes. When Elizabeth's son Brian grew out of the foster home system, we found him and groomed him to join us. He grew to hate you as much as we did. Mary grew very fond of him, and then he was taken from her as well, by another Blanchet. She was so upset that I agreed to go with her and steal his body from the morgue so we could bury him. The idea of him being cut apart in an autopsy was unbearable to her. The pain of losing another person close to her, plus the knowledge that the police were closing in on her, forced her to take her own life. So now it's just me left, and I know my time is running short." Just then a text beeped on Emmie's phone. "Ignore that!" Raj barked.

Glancing down she saw it was Joel. "If I don't answer this, it will create questions," she pleaded.

Raj stared at her for a second, and replied, "Fine send something back to get rid of whoever it is. But let me see it before you send."

Nodding, Emmie texted: "With my friend Julie." Raj snatched the phone out of her hand, glanced at it, and nodded his approval for her to send.

A few minutes later, after more ranting from Raj, Emmie's phone again alerted a text. It was from Sarah this time, asking if there were any updates. Hovering over her, Raj once more demanded that she get rid of the messenger. Emmie texted back a simple "no" before he snatched the phone from her and threw it onto the desk. Raj grabbed a couple of zip ties from his back pocket and pointing the gun closely at Emmie, demanded that she tie her father to the chair.

André spoke up, "mon ami, you do not have to do this! We can talk about it."

Raj shouted in rage, "The time for fucking talking is over, my FRIEND." Turning to Emmie, he snarled, "Tie his hands, or I will blow his brains out right now!" Holding her hands in front of her showing peace and compliance, she fastened her father's hands behind him. Raj gestured for her to return to her seat, and then went to check the ties for secureness. Turning back to Emmie, he sneered, "After killing Brian, when you were in the hospital, I was told that your hunky forest ranger boyfriend made a snide remark about Darwin and survival of fittest. Well, he was right, but not in the way he intended. The fittest *do* survive, which is why I am still here but you two will be dead in a couple of minutes." Turning to André, he gloatingly remarked, "I have waited for this moment for so many years, that I am beyond excited. All that time, pretending to care about you and your family, pretending to be your daughter's faithful employee. The hate I have for you consumes me. I get such joy right now, knowing that there is nothing left you can take from me, but I will now be able to take everything from you. You are going to sit there helplessly while I mutilate and destroy your daughter in ways that will make the surrogate victims look like they had a slap on the wrist." He pointed the gun straight at André as he walked behind Emmie's chair and deftly bound her hands, making her immovable. He walked over to where his jacket was hanging on a coat tree and pulled out a scalpel. "I think first I will start with this pretty little face," he laughed as he walked toward her. Emmie could feel every muscle in her body tense. Her heart was pounding in her ears as he neared her.

Suddenly, there was a crashing sound, as the door crashed off its hinges from the force of a battering ram. "FREEZE!" Shouted the SWAT officers, with their guns pointed. Raj turned to them, grinned defiantly, and raised his pistol toward André. There was the roar of a dozen rifles firing at once, and Raj fell to the floor, riddled with bullet holes. Joel ran past the officers and quickly cut the ties of both Emmie and her father, then swept her into his arms. Softly he whispered to her, "It is over my darling, it is over."

Chapter 25

Emmie, Joel and André gathered in their favorite neighborhood bar, nestled in a corner booth. The trio had spent several hours being debriefed and interviewed and were finally told they could go home and relax. They were all on their third drink and were now starting to feel de-stressed. Suddenly, a figure stood by the table, and Captain Whitaker asked, "May I join you? I was told you were here." The group welcomed him and scooted over to make room. With whiskey in hand, he announced, "I would like to make a toast to some of the finest bunch of people I have had the honor of working with. I am very glad that you are OK. But what I want to know is, Joel how did you find these two?"

Joel smiled and explained, "Well, when I texted Emmie, and she replied that she was with her friend Julie, that was my red flag. You see, she had told me about this friend, who had died when they were kids in a drowning accident. That is how I knew she was in trouble, but I didn't know where she was. I was frantic, I tell ya! But I knew that Sarah was a computer whiz, so I called her and told her the story. She sent Emmie a text and then was able to ping her reply, showing the location. Sarah was then able to send out the troops. But I tell you, it makes my heart stop when I think about how we didn't have a second to spare!"

Whitaker nodded grimly, and mumbled, "Well you are a smart bunch, I will give ya that."

André put his hand to hear mockingly, and asked, "What was that? Didn't hear you. Say it again."

Whitaker laughed and said, "Yea, you wiseass, I had gotten used to your ugly puss!"

The group laughed, then André remarked, "Emmie knows this, but you two don't. My favorite movie of all time, I must have watched it a hundred times, is Casablanca. And my favorite quote is one that I am using for you two men right now…'I believe this may be the beginning of a beautiful friendship'." Laughter ensued as the men raised their glasses to toast. As Whitaker and André began bantering about police work, Joel pulled Emmie in closer to him, and whispered in her ear, "Friendship? I believe, this is the beginning of something much more."

CPSIA information can be obtained
at www.ICGtesting.com
Printed in the USA
BVHW031018161222
654409BV00011B/273